LAST WILL AND TESTAMENT

I, Jason Moorland, being of sound mind, bequeath to my beloved wife, Tracy, along with my other properties, partial ownership of my Montana ranch, the Double J. Because of a debt to Mr. Slade Dawson, the other half of the property title is bequeathed to him. All plans for the estate will be made only with the consent of both owners. This is the least that I owe him after all the suffering he's gone through.

Goodbye, my dear. I wish you all the joy and happiness possible in the years ahead of you. But good luck in getting along with Slade; a more ornery and stubborn young man I've never met!

Please address questions and book requests to: Silhouette Reader Service
U.S.: 3010 Walden Ave., P.O. Box 1325, Buffalo, NY 14269
Canadian: P.O. Box 609, Fort Erie, Ont. L2A 5X3

WESTERN *Lovers*™

JACKIE MERRITT

BIG SKY COUNTRY

Silhouette® Books

Published by Silhouette Books

America's Publisher of Contemporary Romance

SILHOUETTE BOOKS

ISBN 0-373-30192-8

BIG SKY COUNTRY

Visit Silhouette at www.eHarlequin.com

Printed in U.S.A.

One

The vibrantly hued orange-and-black helicopter dipped to the right for its passenger's benefit, and pilot Brock McFee, owner of McFee's Charter Service, jerked his thumb downward. "There it is, ma'am," he yelled over the racket of the engine. "That's the Double J."

Tracy Moorland nodded, her honey-brown curls bouncing, and scanned the toylike buildings and small cattle and horses below. The helicopter went in fast, bringing the ground up at a dizzying speed, turning the miniatures to reality. It had been an incredibly exciting ride, Tracy admitted to herself, her pulse racing. She was glad she'd chosen McFee's Charter Service to cover the hundred miles from the airport in Helena to the Double J Ranch. She was exhausted from a month's hard air travel, and the thought of renting a car and driving a hundred miles had just been too much. This stop was the last leg of a long journey, and Tracy planned to make it short and sweet. She had already made arrangements to phone McFee, probably sometime tomorrow, the next day at the latest, for a return trip.

Tracy spotted men gravitating toward the open space where McFee had chosen to set down. Everything was so green in this valley, she noticed admiringly. The land looked like an enormous, verdant carpet, which was surprising, because they'd passed over so many miles of what appeared to be dry sage and barrenness. The Double J certainly wasn't barren. Far from it. Framed by distant blue-green mountains, the valley contained lush fields, some divided by white-painted fencing. There, sleek reddish horses grazed, and behind white barns, grassy pastureland, dotted with what had to be thousands of head of cattle, seemed to go on forever. Off by itself, only partially visible behind a barrier of massive leaf trees, must be the house, Tracy decided, peering at the little she could see of a white structure with a slate-gray roof.

With a controlled maneuver, McFee swung the helicopter around, and all at once—or so it seemed to Tracy—they were down, settled and stable on the ground. McFee snapped a few switches and the noise abated abruptly, diminishing to the mere slap of the rotor blades. "How'd you like the ride?" he asked with a grin.

Tracy smiled. "It was wonderful." She looked outside at a group of men gathering nearby. "Looks like I have a welcoming committee."

"It's not every day one of these birds land in your front yard," Brock pointed out as he unhooked his safety belt. "But these guys look unusually surprised. Didn't they know you were coming?"

"No, I'm afraid not," Tracy murmured, wondering if maybe the method of her arrival wasn't a bit dramatic, given the circumstance of her visit. No one *did* know she was coming. She'd done it that way purposely, just as she had on each of her other stops. But driving up quietly and introducing herself was a far cry from dropping out of the sky. With a bunch of men gawking to see who was in the helicopter, Tracy was suddenly uncomfortable. Perhaps a car would have been better. She groped for the safety belt catch, which Brock impudently reached over to release for her.

Tracy noted that Brock McFee was young enough to appreciate her looks and brash enough to show it. She hadn't the least problem interpreting his admiring glance—she was no stranger to masculine approval—and she returned the young pilot's hopeful grin with a cool, "sorry, no deal" smile. Brock chuckled and shrugged, obviously accepting the turndown with good humor. He pushed the door open, jumped to the ground and walked around the helicopter.

Tracy turned to look at the scene while she waited, as curious as the men who stood just out of range of the blades. Obviously ranch hands; they were all dressed the same way, in jeans, boots and big hats.

Her gaze swept along, then stopped. A very tall man, his face hidden in the shadow of his hat, seemed to stand out from the rest. It was because of his build, Tracy decided immediately, taking in the lithe ranginess of broad shoulders and slim hips, of long muscular legs that faded denim only enhanced. But several of the other men were well built. This man's stance separated him from the others, belligerent, coldly authoritative, a pose that was at once casual and guarded.

The door swung open, and McFee guided Tracy down. "Careful," he cautioned as she climbed out of the helicopter. With her low-heeled pumps now firmly on the ground, Tracy drew a deep breath and smiled tentatively at the staring men. Just then a woman at least twenty years older than Tracy, who was twenty-eight, ran up and stopped beside the harsh-looking man Tracy had scrutinized.

Aware that the pilot was pulling her luggage from the helicopter, Tracy started walking toward the silent group, naturally drawn to the woman. "Hello," she called before reaching her.

The woman stepped forward. "Hello," she said in a friendly way. Tracy relaxed somewhat, noting the woman's lively, warm features, her ample figure, clothed in a green cotton housedress, the gray in her dark hair. But if the woman looked welcoming, no one else did. Especially, Tracy realized, that impressive hunk of lanky masculinity. It was obvious from his air of ownership and from the darting glances the other men kept throwing him—as if they were all waiting to see what he would do—that he was the boss of the Double J.

Tracy held her hand out. "I'm Tracy Moorland," she said calmly, "Mrs. Jason Moorland."

The smile faded from the woman's face, and Tracy was sure her hostess lost at least three shades of color. She seemed instantly confused. Ignoring Tracy's outstretched hand, she turned to the tall man. Feeling foolish, Tracy let her hand fall to her side, aware that the man was moving forward.

"You're who?" The words were spit out, clipped, harsh.

"I'm Tracy Moorland," she repeated, wondering what was going on. At all her other stops on this trip, she'd been greeted with almost embarrassing deference. What was wrong here? It was not that she wanted to be fawned over, but she at least expected common courtesy.

The man was close enough now for her to make out his face beneath the wide-brimmed hat. Cold gray eyes stared at her insolently, and Tracy felt a flush begin at her toes and finally reach her cheeks in a wave of crimson. Somehow, despite her embarrassment, she was able to assess his features. He wasn't handsome. Strangely, his too-square jaw, the grim set of his lips, a nose that wasn't very straight, made her feel better.

Abruptly the man swung around. "Everyone back to work," he snapped. "The show's over."

Tracy watched as the men left, talking among themselves and glancing back at her, still obviously very curious. Brock McFee came up to her. "Everything's unloaded, Mrs. Moorland. I'll be waiting for your call."

"Thank you." Her attention riveted on the tall man, Tracy was vaguely aware of Brock returning to the helicopter. "I'm sure my arriving in this manner was a bit surprising—" she began.

The woman hadn't left with everyone else, and she gave the tall man what was clearly a disapproving glance. "I'm Rachel Munley, Mrs. Moorland. Welcome to the Double J."

"Thank you," Tracy said, breathing a small sigh of relief. Her green eyes moved to the man again.

Rachel spoke up. "Slade, let's take Mrs. Moorland's luggage to the house."

"I'd rather she got back in that machine and got the hell out of here," he snarled, giving Tracy another cold stare.

Behind them, the helicopter's engine started and the accelerating rotor blades sent a blast of wind in their direction. Tracy was shocked by the man's rudeness. She was almost frightened, and she darted fretful glances at the two strangers watching her. The man's gray eyes contained open hostility, and Rachel Munley's expression remained uneasy. Suddenly the helicopter took off. When it was out of sight the air calmed, relieving the physical turbulence around them.

In the ensuing quiet, hardly able to believe she was being treated so badly, Tracy began to get angry. She was here, dammit, and only because the Double J was on the list. A ranch in Montana was the last place she'd have wanted to visit otherwise. This rude individual could like it or lump it. It was all the same to her. "As you can see, that machine is gone," she said sarcastically. "Maybe I should speak frankly," she continued firmly. "I own half of this ranch and intend to see it." She looked directly into Slade's icy gray eyes. "From your patronizing attitude, I suspect you're my partner. Am I right?"

Slade didn't flinch. He knew nothing in his face gave away his thoughts, but privately he was seething. The Moorland name was enough to do it, but to have that name attached to this woman, a woman who couldn't be more than twenty-five or twenty-six, made his blood boil. Her good looks grated, too. Her hair was the color of good whiskey, and those green eyes—hell, who had green eyes? She was impossibly pretty, with a lush body and expensive clothes.

He smirked bitterly. "You got it, lady. I'm your partner, all right."

Tracy stared. "Would it be asking too much to know your name?"

Now he'd get a reaction. His name would no doubt shock her socks off, just as hers had him. The barest hint of cynical amusement showed on his lips. "Slade Dawson," he replied.

"Well, Mr. Dawson, like it or not, I plan to take a look at the Double J."

Slade looked at Rachel and saw by her expression that she was thinking the same thing he was. His name hadn't meant a thing to Tracy Moorland. She didn't know. An odd feeling of relief hit him, and he was able to say in a slightly less menacing voice, "Look all you want to. No one around here gives a damn." Pivoting with the grace of a panther, he strode over to her pile of luggage. "How in hell long are you planning to look, though? There's enough damn luggage here for an army."

Lord, he was rude! Tracy thought as she moved to the stack of suitcases. "I've been on an extended trip," she said coldly. "This is my last stop."

"Thank God for small favors," Slade muttered, grabbing a suitcase and tucking it under one arm, then picking up two others. He took off without looking back.

Retrieving her cosmetic bag, Tracy reached for the last suitcase. "Let me, Mrs. Moorland," Rachel said, taking it from her. "Come along up to the house. You must be tired."

"Thank you, Rachel. I am," Tracy admitted wearily. "Please call me Tracy," she said as they walked in the direction Slade was going at such a fast pace. He was way ahead of them and increasing the distance between them with every long step. "Is he always so cordial?"

"Slade is…just Slade," Rachel murmured quietly. "He's a good man."

Tracy doubted the "good" but there was no doubt Slade Dawson was a man. He exuded masculinity, and despite his rudeness—and his crooked nose—he was enough to draw any woman's notice. Well, she wouldn't be around long enough to find out for herself if the man had any "good" points. And, frankly, she couldn't care less. She was tired and just plain anxious to get this final stop out of the way so she could go home.

Home. The word brought an odd tangle of emotions with it. Home was merely a word these days, one that conjured up the loveliness of the elegant Marin County house and grounds, to be sure, but also one that contained an emptiness that was impossible to ignore. Ever since Jase's death, the home they had shared for four years hadn't had much meaning.

Perhaps she'd taken this trip just to get out of that silent house, Tracy mused, although she'd certainly thought it imperative to see for herself what she'd inherited. Jase had been an extraordinarily private man and had only rarely mentioned business to her. Taking over the management of a virtual empire of real estate holdings scattered in a dozen different areas had been a massive endeavor. After a year of dealing with figures and reports, she had decided to personalize the information by viewing her holdings firsthand. Thus far, the trip had been extremely satisfying. Here at the Double J, however, she felt like an intruder, and it was very unnerving.

They were passing through the grove of trees protecting the house, and the sudden cooler temperature felt wonderful, making Tracy realize just how warm it had been in the open. "These trees look old," she remarked, glancing up at their enormous gnarled branches. "What are they?"

"Cottonwoods, mostly. They shade the house real nice all summer."

Tracy could see that the cottonwoods surrounded the house on all sides, even the front, though a wide expanse of neatly trimmed lawn separated the foliage from the building. Flower beds boasted colorful petunias and marigolds, and the house, though obviously old, looked to be in good repair, strong and sturdy. The feature that made the house unique, Tracy noted approvingly, were the double porches running the full width of the house, providing both first- and second-floor balconies. "I'm not sure what I expected to see on a Montana ranch," Tracy admitted. "But I don't think this is it."

Rachel laughed. "Have you always lived in a city?"

"Yes, in San Francisco."

They ascended the porch stairs. "You'll find life here a lot different, Tracy, but you might like it."

"I probably won't be here long enough to find out," Tracy replied, following Rachel into a large, cool foyer. Highly polished hardwood flooring adorned with striking, colorful woven rugs greeted her curious eyes. "This is charming."

"The bedrooms are upstairs," Rachel informed her, heading for a wide, curving staircase. "Let's get you settled. Then you can take a tour of the house."

Boots thumping down the stairs drew Tracy's gaze upward. Slade was coming toward her, still glowering, still with that look on his face that sent a skittering prickle up her spine. It was obvious he resented her being here, which seemed so senseless to her. Why should he care? With Jase gone, Slade must have known that one day he'd have to meet his current partner. And there certainly was nothing strange about that partner being Jason Moorland's wife. What was Slade Dawson, some kind of woman-hater, naturally put out at having an unplanned-for female partner?

Even in the house, his hat remained firmly in place, Tracy noted. Angry at the man's lack of good manners, Tracy still wondered what was under that cockily set Stetson. Maybe he was losing his hair, she hoped with a jab of something close to hatred, although from the thick dark hair brushing the collar of his blue chambray shirt, she doubted it.

He was going to pass them without even speaking! Maybe poor Rachel was used to such treatment, but she wasn't. She'd force him to speak, to acknowledge that she was there. She'd relish his discomfort, too. "Thank you for taking my luggage up." Boldly, Tracy moved into his path. "My stay here will last as long as it takes to inspect the ranch, Mr. Dawson." Out of the corner of her eye Tracy caught a silent but vivid warning from Rachel. Clearly the woman thought her demented to as much as ask for Slade's wrath.

Well, she wasn't afraid of this cretin. She had as much right to be on the Double J as Slade Dawson. "So maybe it would benefit both of us if you'd be a little less antagonistic," she said clearly.

Gray eyes that were already cold and unfriendly

narrowed even more. "Is that a fact?" Slade spit out. Behind him, Tracy caught Rachel's aghast expression, and she wasn't surprised when she scurried on up the stairs and disappeared. "I don't know what you're doing here, and I don't want to know. Take your 'look' and get the hell off the Double J!"

"I have a right to be here," she exclaimed heatedly. "Just who do you think you are? You don't own one blade of grass here that isn't half mine." The fact that he was standing three steps above her made him look like a giant. As the adrenaline of a fast and overwhelming anger pumped feverishly through her system, Tracy became aware of the hard ridges of his belly beneath his taut chambray shirt. She realized she was in a debasing position and hastened to remedy it by climbing up to occupy the same step as he. "I'll stay as long as I want to stay," she declared vehemently.

"So stay, dammit! But don't bother me. Just keep out of my way!" With a look that Tracy thought probably had the power to cow strong men, Slade tramped down the stairs. Tracy heard the front door slam hard enough that the whole house reverberated.

Tracy stared blankly, her anger gradually replaced by disbelief. Was the man insane? Numbly she started up the stairs again, deeply confused. Why would he object so strenuously to her presence? Slade Dawson acted as if he actually despised her, but why should he? They'd never met before. In fact, until Jason's death and the long, arduous conferences with his attorneys and accountants, she hadn't even known the

Double J existed. She hadn't known about any of the properties she now owned: apartment complexes, office buildings, real estate in a dozen different cities. True, a ranch among all those urban developments had made her wonder, but no more than everything else had. Jase had successfully kept the extent of his financial empire from her. She would never know why, and she had stopped worrying about it, though when she'd first learned of the complexities of her inheritance it had nearly driven her crazy.

Rachel met her in the hall. "Leave Slade be," she said quietly. "My brother Ben works on the ranch, and I'll get him to show you around." She gestured toward an open door. "Here's your room."

Tracy found the large room immediately appealing. She saw high ceilings, a fireplace, white lace curtains and old-fashioned, heavy wooden furniture, all of it spotlessly clean and comfortable-looking. The peace of the room drained some of her tension. She drew a deep breath and relaxed. "It's nice, Rachel. Thanks."

Slade apparently forgotten, Rachel bustled over to the French windows and, to Tracy's delight, pulled them open, revealing the balcony. "You can sleep with these doors open; it's perfectly safe," Rachel assured her. Tracy stepped outside. The balcony, as she'd noticed earlier, ran the full width of the house. Two other doors opened onto it, also.

"The house is old and only has two bathrooms," Rachel said. "Come along and I'll show you where they are."

Tracy nodded, slightly reluctant to leave the balcony, and followed Rachel's sturdy figure. She wanted to ask about Slade and his ridiculous dislike of her but had a feeling Rachel wouldn't give her much information. Although she sensed Rachel liked her, her first loyalty was rightfully to Slade.

After pointing out the bathrooms and the linen cupboards, Rachel said, "I'll leave you to get settled now, Tracy. Dinner is at six, but if you want anything before then, just come down to the kitchen." She stared to walk away. "Just poke around yourself if you want to see the rest of the house, or give a yell and I'll be glad to show it to you."

"Thank you. I think I'd like a bath and maybe a little nap right now."

"Good enough. See you later."

Returning to the big bedroom, Tracy closed the door and eyed the suitcases in the middle of the floor. It was certain she didn't need to unpack them, not for a two-day stay. Considering Slade Dawson's miserably uncooperative attitude, she should stay a month. It would serve him right. The man was impossible. She'd never met a harder, more unlikable man in her life.

Nor one with a better body, an inner voice added. Well, that was true, Tracy conceded reluctantly. He did have an incredible body, muscle and bone and hard flesh in all the right places, and not one ounce of fat. Like cold steel, she thought grimly as she pulled her blouse off, recalling eyes that mirrored that description to perfection. Slade Dawson's face was nothing to get excited about, though, Tracy exulted.

Not at all like Jase's handsome, suave features. She dug out a robe and slipped it on, grabbed her cosmetic bag and went down the hall to the nearest bathroom.

Flipping the lock, Tracy filled the old-fashioned marble tub. Within minutes the scent and liquid silk of a soothing bubble bath were so relaxing that she put her head back and closed her eyes with a contented sigh. It was an odd feeling to be in a ranch house in Montana, but then her trip had taken her to a lot of places she'd never been: Chicago, Miami, Houston. Her travels had left her with a strange sense of rootlessness. She'd planned her itinerary to make the Double J her last stop, and at times had even contemplated omitting it, wondering over and over again about the anomaly of there being a cattle ranch among Jason's holdings.

No man could have been farther removed from the earthiness and physicality of a ranch than Jase. Now that she had met her husband's partner, his ownership of the place utterly amazed her. How had Jase met a man like Slade Dawson and formed such an unlikely partnership? It wasn't just the disparity in their ages that made the liaison improbable, though Jase had certainly been much older than Slade appeared to be. No, it was more the memory of Jase's smooth, urbane personality, his disdain for anything but the very best, his cultural snobbishness, that perplexed Tracy. Jase wouldn't have given the time of day to a man like Slade. She'd lived with her late husband's arrogance for four years, and she knew Jase and Slade could never have been friends.

Maybe Slade and Jase had had enough antagonism between them to carry over to her. She pondered the possibility, which made as much sense as anything else, she decided. "Well, Mr. Dawson, you're just going to have to put up with me for a few days whether you like it or not," she murmured aloud, standing up in the tub and reaching for the towel.

The bathroom door burst open with the impact of a tornado. Tracy's gasp was lost in her haste to cover herself, and she paid for her nervousness by dropping the towel. Numbly she stared at the sinking terry cloth, stunned to immobility. Slade stood there, frozen, as surprised as she. "Sorry," he muttered, though he made no move to leave. His gray eyes washed over her, lingering on the swells of perfect breasts, rosy nipples upright with tension, and long, sensuous thighs. She was beautiful, the most beautiful woman he'd ever seen, and he couldn't stop looking.

Tracy's gaze darted around the room. The water was gurgling down the drain, and she'd placed only one towel within reach. Her robe hung on a hook behind the door, out of sight—and Slade just kept staring. "You *could* leave!" she flung out harshly.

"I could," he agreed softly, "but you're the sweetest looking thing I've ever seen."

Waves of heat reddened Tracy and, wondering wildly why she hadn't done it before, she retrieved the soaked towel and held it in front of herself. "Get out of here," she snapped. Slade's shirt was unbuttoned, and a mass of dark hair covered his chest. He wasn't even slightly bald, Tracy realized dimly, seeing his thick, tousled hair, unbrushed, untamed, set free from that infernal hat.

"If you don't want company," Slade drawled, taking advantage of the situation to the last second by studying her intently, seeing through the cling of white terry, admiring what was still bare, her lightly tanned shoulders, the slope of breasts visible above the towel. "You might try locking the door."

"I thought I did!" Tracy hurled. She swore she heard a soft laugh as the door finally swung shut and a debilitating weakness brought her head down. Oh, Lord, what a moment! She wanted to feel defiled, insulted. Instead, she was furious with herself because she didn't. Those gray eyes on her, staring, penetrating, roaming every inch of her body—it was the most erotic thing that had ever happened to her. She tingled, she glowed, and feelings she'd thought she'd buried with Jase were buffeting her with relentless fury.

The memory of four years of a satisfying life with a man she'd loved suddenly devoured her, and for the first time in a year she suffered the intense ache of abstinence. The thought that it was because of a rude, crude, insolent man like Slade Dawson made her ill. Her hands shook so hard that it was a struggle to dry herself off and put her robe on.

She slammed out of the bathroom, close to tears, and stopped short. Slade was leaning in the doorway of the room next to hers, a cynical look on his face. "All through…bathing?" he asked, the simple question filled with innuendo.

Her face flaming, Tracy turned and ran. When she was in her room, with the door securely locked, she heard her fast, unsteady breathing filled with panic. Could she be attracted to that lout? Impossible! Yet she couldn't forget his eyes on her, couldn't forget the image of him standing there with his shirt unbuttoned, with all that black hair on his bronzed chest, hair that narrowed to a fine line that dipped into his jeans.

And what had made her think his face wasn't handsome? True, it wasn't even-featured as Jase's had been, but dear Lord, Slade Dawson's face conveyed so much machismo and rugged maleness, it would haunt her the rest of her life.

When Tracy went downstairs two hours later, she was still shaken. Leery of seeing Slade again, she was relieved when Rachel said he wouldn't be home for dinner. "He went to town," the genial housekeeper informed her. "Ben eats with us, though, so you can ask him about showing you around tomorrow."

"Thank you, I'll do that," Tracy murmured feebly. Ignoring the strange look Rachel gave her at the tremulous thinness in her voice, she went outside to take a walk before dinner. With Slade gone to "town," wherever that might be, she felt free to wander and ended up at one of the white fences she'd seen from the air. About thirty graceful roan horses grazed inside the compound, and Tracy leaned on the fence and watched them for a long time. A few of them lifted their heads and stared at her curiously when she first came along, but after a short while they paid her no mind.

What an utterly beautiful spot, Tracy thought, basking in the peace and quiet, the clean air, the odd sense of feeling far removed from the six o'clock news and all the horrors it encompassed. "A person could easily get addicted to this," she murmured softly. Then she remembered that even in this pastoral paradise, a "snake in the grass" lurked—Slade Dawson.

As Tracy gazed at the splendid animals beyond the fence, she realized it would be extremely wise to make a quick inspection tomorrow and leave the Double J posthaste—while she still could. She was no match for this particular serpent, not when she was already branded with an unforgettable memory. And he hadn't even touched her! Hanging around to see what might come next was asking for something she might not be able to handle. Might not be able to handle? Tracy laughed humorlessly. That was the understatement of the year!

Two

Shorty's Bar and Grill was Tuesday-night quiet, with only a few regulars perched on their favorite stools. These old-timers didn't much care what night of the week it was. They were as much a part of the landscape as the egg-shell cartoned ceiling and the silver dollars embedded in the surface of the bar. Slade finished his second beer and called for another. He didn't intend to get stewed, but getting off the ranch and away from that woman had been necessary.

Tracy Moorland, his dear departed father's wife. What a laugh! Hell, she was young enough to be Jason Moorland's daughter. What had she done, married the old geezer for his money? Slade reached for the bottle that Buck, the bartender, had set down and refilled his glass, watching the foam develop. His thick eyebrows were drawn together in a dark glower that effectively forestalled Buck's usual convivial commentary.

Downing a third of the glass's icy liquid, Slade wiped his mouth with the back of his hand. He'd known for a year that the man who had biologically fathered him was dead, but nothing on earth could have prevented the tearing shock of suddenly facing his widow. *Why* was she here? After all these years, why was a Moorland suddenly interested in the Double J? As far as Slade knew, Jason Moorland had never set foot on the ranch. Now, without warning, and with all the impact of an atom bomb, his widow showed up.

The questions burned him with fiery intensity, dredging up painful memories, old sorrows he'd spent most of his life trying to forget. What would his mother say if she were still alive? Imagine if Jemma Dawson were still living today and Tracy had barged in the way she had! Slade's guts churned with bitterness at the thought, with a renewal of the hatred he'd grown up with and had hoped was behind him, hatred for a man he'd never met—Jason Moorland.

Tracy hadn't batted an eye when she'd heard Slade's name. So, for some unimaginable reason, Jason Moorland hadn't told his wife about the son he'd never claimed. Slade smirked silently, staring at the amber bubbles in his glass, pondering the whys of Jason Moorland. What could have made the man cold and unfeeling enough to desert a pregnant woman, then turn around and, for some dark, unfathomable reason, buy a ranch like the Double J and give her half of it?

Every time he let himself dig into his past and try to make sense of it, Slade was stopped by a morass of emotional loose ends, things he'd never know the reasons for. Jemma had told him her side when he'd been fourteen and hungry for knowledge of who and what he was. He'd already been weary of having no name other than "Dawson," which he knew full well was his mother's maiden name. That day, in a painfully low voice, her face white and deathly still, his mother had explained her mistake, how she had loved—and lost.

Cursing under his breath, Slade ripped his thoughts away from that still-debilitating memory, zeroing in again on Tracy and the rationale behind her visit. Without trying, he also remembered the water sliding down her gleaming body, the shock he'd felt when he'd pushed the bathroom door open and seen her in the tub. His body stirred convulsively in an unwanted reaction to the memory of that tantalizing female flesh. Disgust with himself for being so weak as to be tempted by her, his father's wife, gripped his vitals.

He *hated* thinking of her, but she remained in his mind, lush and ripe and ready for some man to take what was so plentiful. Slade upended the glass, seeking to quench the flame in his gut. Its hot tentacles were reaching, seeping, threatening to consume everything in their path—conscious thought, reason, clarity. He had to stay alert, to put Tracy Moorland's considerable charms aside and concentrate on protecting the Double J. It was everything to him, and the only thing that had any meaning for him. Maybe in some intangible way, he'd always known the day would come when he'd have to face a threat to his ownership.

Not even in his wildest fantasies could he have dreamed the threat might arrive in the form of a beautiful, sexy woman. When, in an impersonal message from the accounting firm handling the ranch's books and records, he'd learned of Jason Moorland's death and been told fifty percent of the Double J's profits would now go to his estate, Slade had relaxed his vigil. His dread that one day Jason Moorland would follow a whim or develop a conscience and want to see the ranch and his son had lessened.

A premature conclusion, Slade admitted wryly. A money-hungry widow might be more of a threat than old Jason had ever been. As a fifty-percent owner, could she bleed the ranch? He'd have to check on just what Tracy could do before he got too worked up. Maybe she was empowered only to sell her share. Slade sat up, excited by the possibility. If that was the case, he'd beg, borrow or steal the money to buy her out. The idea of hundred-percent ownership was too thrilling to dwell on; a distant dream that he feared hoping for would jinx.

Still, the next few days loomed direly. With all that luggage and a weak story about having been on a long trip, Slade doubted Tracy only intended staying a short time. She had enough with her to move in, and the prospect of tripping over her every few hours was damned disturbing.

All right, he silently admitted, maybe I would like to feel that luscious body under me. Hell, a man would have to be made of stone not to be affected by that scene in the bathroom.

And he wasn't anywhere near made of stone, though it might be a helpful condition in dealing with the beauteous Mrs. Moorland.

Slade wondered if he could pull it off now that he'd had a long look and knew what no amount of expensive clothing would be able to conceal. Could he look her in the eye and hide what he would doubtless be thinking?

On the other hand, maybe that gave him an edge. If she had the slightest inclination toward modesty, wouldn't she be uncomfortable around him? A cynical smile softened the grimness of his face. Maybe he was going at this all wrong. Maybe Tracy wouldn't be at all averse to a little playing around.

Wouldn't that be an ironic private revenge on the man who'd caused his mother so much pain and who'd denied his son until the day he died? It was such a satisfying idea that Slade chuckled softly, acknowledging that the satisfaction would be doubly enjoyable. Having Tracy Moorland would not only heal a lot of old wounds, it just might be the most physically exhilarating experience of his life.

With a sardonic laugh, he slid off the stool and tossed some bills on the bar. "See you, Buck," he called as he ambled the length of the bar and headed for the door.

"So long, Slade." Buck's answer was barely noticed as Slade stepped into the night.

It was warm, a beautiful, balmy night, and it was later than Slade had thought. Looking at his watch, he was surprised to see it was nearly eleven. After leaving the ranch, he'd driven around for a long time, thinking, killing time, anything to avoid the evening meal and sitting down at the table with that woman. Everyone would be in bed now. He could return without worrying about running into her.

Tracy turned over in the unfamiliar bed and opened her eyes. A noise in the otherwise quiet night had awakened her. Moonlight streamed through the open French doors, bathing the room in silvery light, delineating the heavy furniture, chasing the inexplicable fear that had gripped her momentarily. She sighed softly, relaxing somewhat and reaching for sleep again. She stretched her legs beneath the sheet, catching the pleasing perfume of growing things, flowers, trees. A far-off cow bawled, and she stirred restlessly, remembering the day again.

With Slade away, the Double J had taken on a whole different aspect. Dinner had been enjoyable. Rachel's brother, Ben, was a likable fellow. About five years younger than Rachel, he had reddish hair and kindly brown eyes. The three of them had talked and visited until after dark, the conversation mostly about the ranch. Rachel had lived on the Double J for over thirty years, and Ben almost ten. It was their home, and they both spoke of it with love and pride.

Ben had promised to escort her around the place in the morning, and Tracy felt a sense of anticipation whenever she thought about it. If only Slade would stay away, she wished ardently. Maybe the bathroom episode had shocked him so much that he didn't want to see her again, either. That seemed pretty unlikely, from the way he'd stood there and taken his sweet time staring.

What a nerve! Any man with an ounce of decency would have slammed the door immediately. Not Slade Dawson, though. She'd never forget the look on his face while those steely gray eyes had roamed. And they hadn't been quite so steely, either, had they? In fact, they'd looked like pure molten lava, and so much heat had emanated from Slade's long, intense scrutiny that Tracy could still feel it.

Suddenly breathless—and blaming the unusually warm night—Tracy slipped out of bed and went to the open doors. The long skirt of her satin nightgown swirled around her ankles, catching moonbeams in the lustrous ice-blue tint. She readjusted one of the tiny straps, which had slipped down a shoulder, exposing the top of a breast. The night breeze beyond the doors was tempting, and she stepped out on the balcony.

"Hmmm," she murmured, raising her face to the breeze and closing her eyes. It felt heavenly. She lifted her heavy hair and held it up to bathe her neck and shoulders in the cooler air. Despite the open doors, the room had been stuffy, and the liquidity of the soft night felt sensuous on her skin. She breathed deeply, feeling the rise of her breasts, her nipples growing taut at the sweet torment of the satin.

Lord, would she never get rid of the mood Slade's slow study had put her in? A seemingly unquenchable fire burned in the pit of her stomach, barely tolerable, irritatingly persistent. She'd slept only fitfully, and who knew what small sound had awakened her? Perhaps it had simply been discord within herself. With an unhappy sigh, Tracy brought her arms down. At that precise moment, she realized she wasn't alone.

Her heart leaped wildly, and she was afraid to search the shadows and see who was there. She turned very slowly, poised to run if need be, her breath choked in her throat. A long, lanky shadow moved, straightened from its slouch along the wall. *Slade!*

It hit her that he'd been watching her, that he'd stood silent and staring again! Had the man no scruples whatsoever? He moved closer, a silent wraith without a shirt, his bare feet taking soundless steps, the features of his craggy face vague in the moonlight. Her heart pounded in her breast. "What are you doing out here?" Her voice sounded hoarse, foreign.

"The same thing you are, getting some air. Too hot to sleep?"

The question was rampant with innuendo. Gratefully Tracy noticed that he was wearing jeans. At first, her senses focused on his bare chest, she'd thought him totally nude. "No," she said quickly, ignoring his double entendre. "Something woke me—a noise."

"That was probably me coming in. I just got back." Slade felt her presence in every cell of his body. She was wispy and unreal in the silvery light. Her slightest movement caused a voluptuous shimmer of pale satin. Held in place by skimpy ribbons over her shoulders, the dainty cups over her breasts barely concealed her full, rounded figure and only enhanced the firmness of her nipples. He stared at them, suddenly aching to touch, to feel, to take.

Tracy knew she should leave. She should return to her own room. He wouldn't dare follow. He towered over her, close enough to touch should she choose, breathing softly but audibly, his chest rising and falling rhythmically. The heat in her body was almost painful. She'd never been so aware of a man before, so physically drawn. Her tongue flicked, wetting her suddenly dry lips. "You missed dinner," she whispered.

Elation drugged Slade. He'd been right. She wasn't a bit averse to playing around. What a laugh on dear old Dad! He hadn't dreamed the opportunity would come so soon to test Tracy's morals, but far be it from him to refuse a lady in obvious distress. Slowly, provocatively, Slade inched closer. He raised one hand to her arm and slid it up the silky skin to her shoulder, feeling her responsive shiver. She was ready, almost panting, for a man. This was going to be easy. "I wasn't hungry then," he whispered, bending forward and pressing his lips to her shoulder, stunned by the impact he felt in his loins.

She smelled sweet, smelled of soap and perfume.

The scent seeped into his senses and curled within him, raising his blood pressure. His mouth moved unhurriedly, clinging to the soft slope of her throat. "I'm hungry now," he whispered, bringing his arms around her and settling her back against them.

Tracy gasped for air. Her head back, her eyes open, she stared at the velvety sky, at the billions of stars watching them. She burned wherever he touched, and she could hardly believe what was happening. Letting a virtual stranger make love to her, let alone one who had nearly snapped her head off earlier, was so different from her normal behavior that a part of her was stunned, shaken. But the part Slade was reaching, that deeply sensuous female side of her, a side she had only suspected before this, was languishing in his arms, responding with more wildness than she'd ever shown Jase. A shudder passed through her small frame as Slade's mouth explored her throat and moved downward, hot and wet, to her breasts.

Her hands came up of their own accord and clasped his head, lingered in the thick, unruly hair there, then moved down the solidity of his neck to his shoulders. Steel, she thought. Slade was made of steel, just as she'd decided before, but she'd been wrong on one point. He definitely was not cold steel. His skin was hot and smooth and sensitized her wandering fingertips to the point of utter wantonness. Without his even having kissed her on the lips, Tracy knew she wanted Slade Dawson in every way possible. She wanted him nude, she wanted to view and explore his incredible body, she wanted him on her, in her. And she wanted his kiss on her mouth. Now. Right this moment.

"Slade..." It was all she needed to say, for that one breathy word contained enough erotic invitation and need to melt an iceberg.

Leaving the nipple he'd been so entranced by, Slade straightened up and pulled her forward, bringing her entire body in pulsing contact with his. That he was fully aroused and thrusting against her made Tracy gasp, perhaps from shock at her own behavior, certainly not from surprise that he was so affected. Slade's arousal only mirrored her own, and even without that blatant proof, she would have known what he was feeling. Without hesitation she raised her arms to his neck and pressed into him, needing this as much as she needed air or water or any other life-sustaining element. Her lips were parted, moist and trembling, waiting for his.

In the moonlight, Slade looked down at her, studied the passion on her face. Something dark and arcane swirled within him, an uneasiness, a sense of daring fate, of meddling in something better left alone. Who would know if he made love to his father's wife? Who was there to laugh and affirm his vengeance with? Rachel? She'd been Jemma's best friend and had lived the painful past with her. Rachel wouldn't laugh. She'd be shocked into speechlessness. Old friends who might remember the tired old story with a reminder? Which of them would care enough to laugh? Ben hadn't been around then, and he only knew whatever Rachel had told him. The lonely truth was, he was the only one who still cared—and he didn't feel much like laughing right now.

The woman in his arms stirred, silently urging him, questioning his hesitation. Was she simply an innocent participant in this most ironic chapter of his life story? Or was she an extremely clever and selfish taker, whether it was a man she wanted or a ranch?

If only she didn't feel so right...

With a guttural groan, he took what she offered, the sweet lips that leaped to life beneath his. It flashed through his mind that his small revenge was backfiring, but in the next beat of his heart it didn't matter. It suddenly didn't matter at all, not who she was or what her motives might be. She was warm and lush, the ultimate female, and his body ached with need of her. His mouth opened wider, taking all of her, devouring the moist curves of her lips, and his arms strove to unite her soft body in a permanent bond with his. He stood taller, lifted her from the balcony floor, inviting her to further intimacy, and his blood roared through his veins when her legs clasped around his hips.

She was willing! More than willing—eager! Passion exploded between them, and the kiss became almost savage. He knew where this was heading. It could only end one way, in her bed or his. Never had he been so consumed by pure, unadulterated wanting. Where had this wild passion come from? She was beautiful, but she wasn't the first beautiful woman he'd known. There was more here than just simple sexual excitement. It had to do with who she was and who he was and…

Lord, could he really do it? Slade broke the kiss and stared into her face, seeing the swollen moistness of her lips, the starlight reflected in eyes dark with need and promise—and an odd surprise. He wondered at the contradiction, at the way she'd led him on, then seemed surprised when he'd heeded the invitation. He wondered, too, that she could be surprised and not try to stop him. What kind of a woman was she?

One for whom making love with a man she hardly knew was a common occurrence?

Something recoiled inside Slade at the thought, something to either be put aside and forgotten forever or faced head-on. It was an odd feeling, the tip of an emotional iceberg, a strange wish that this woman who fit in his arms as though designed for him could be someone other than who she was.

For a moment he was still, his rasping breath shattering the night quiet, his arms supporting her and holding her close to him. Tracy returned his probing gaze, seeing something in his face that began to seep through the hot clouds gripping her mind. She couldn't quite understand his expression, yet she sensed reluctance, a holding back. Quite suddenly the reality of what she was doing gripped her. Had she lost her mind completely?

"Put me down," she whispered thickly, so humiliated that she was thankful it was dark enough to partially conceal her embarrassment. He hesitated, and she felt his big hands cupping the curves of her buttocks, burning her skin through the flimsy gown. "Please," she added in a hoarse, unnatural voice.

She wouldn't have stopped him if he hadn't delayed, he realized darkly. She had wanted exactly what he had, to see this through to what had promised to be an incredible fulfillment. He could still sense her need, but now it was buried, tucked away behind a beautiful face that showed only the wish that she could undo the last few minutes.

Slowly he let her feet slide to the balcony floor, but he kept her close, unwilling to release her completely. He stared down at her, seeing a tear glisten in the corner of one eye, wondering what kind of fool he really was. He could have been in her bed by now. It would have been so easy just to carry her into her room.

Tracy's hands moved from his shoulders to the strong, muscular arms around her. Her heart was thumping so hard that she could hear it pounding in her ears. "Please let me go," she whispered. She wanted to ask how this had happened. What spell had he cast over her to make her want him with such an uncontrollable need and to forget anything else existed? Nothing even remotely like this had ever happened to her before, and she didn't understand it.

But neither had it ever happened to Slade. What was tearing him apart as he stole another moment next to her was that just because his damned thoughts had slowed his progress didn't mean his blood had cooled. It was all too apparent that no matter who this woman was, she had managed to get under his skin.

He still wanted her, and there were all kinds of crazy, mixed-up emotions involved in that desire.

If she weren't Tracy Moorland she would be exactly the kind of woman he could fall for, he realized darkly.

Abruptly he dropped his hands and stepped back. "Go on back to bed," he growled, angrier with himself than with her.

Tracy reeled at suddenly finding herself unsupported. The absence of Slade's warm, hard body left her strangely bereft, and she reached for the balcony rail reflexively. "This...this never should have happened," she whispered huskily.

"You bet your sweet life it shouldn't have. Don't worry, it won't happen again." So much for revenge, he thought sardonically. Talk about a stupid idea jumping up and kicking a man where it hurt most!

He regarded Tracy, noticing the slight trembling in her body. Why didn't she go? What did she want now, conversation? Slade grimaced. They had nothing to talk about, and they never would. "Go to bed, Mrs. Moorland," he said gruffly.

It was certain he wasn't going to apologize, Tracy thought. She hadn't really expected him to, had she? This had been no more his fault than hers, anyway. Maybe there'd been something wild and hot between them at first glance. Maybe that was why there had been all those sparks.

Lord, she really had lost her mind. Sighing, Tracy turned away. "Good night," she murmured.

Slade never answered, but he remained on the balcony long after Tracy was out of sight. He had a lot to think about. How long was she going to hang around? Maybe it would be best if he got off the ranch for a few days. If she'd been telling the truth about the length of time she intended to stay, she could take her look without his presence and be gone before he got back.

One thing was certain: he didn't want a repeat of tonight's performance. And he wasn't at all sure he could keep his hands off her if he stayed on the ranch, especially if she invited him again as she had done tonight.

Tracy lay awake for hours. The open French doors were like gates to heaven or hell, she wasn't sure which. But the intense sensuality she'd experienced in Slade Dawson's arms was one or the other. She wasn't entirely positive she'd say no if he suddenly appeared within that starlit frame.

Maybe she even wished he would.

"Oh, damn," she whispered, hardly able to believe she'd behaved so disgustingly. How could a normal, moral woman meet a man and suddenly lose all her sense of decency? It just wasn't possible.

All her life Tracy had lived one way, with a rather rigid moral code. At twenty-two, when she'd met Jason Moorland, she'd still been a virgin. Perhaps she'd been an oddity by today's relaxed standards, but it was true nonetheless. While she stared into the unfamiliar, moonlit room, time scampered through

Tracy's mind, memories of meeting Jase, his court-ship, their life together.

Actually, it was her father who had introduced them. Jim Kirkland was a loan officer in a bank, a reasonably successful man, and as such he had many friends in the business world. Tracy had not been long out of college, busy with a burgeoning career in her chosen field of computer science and enjoying a new level of independence. She had had her own apart-ment but had seen her father often, meeting him every Thursday for lunch. One such Thursday, Jim had brought Jason Moorland.

Tracy was positive her father had never once thought of her and Jase as a match. After all, Jason Moorland had been more than thirty years her senior. Her father couldn't have anticipated his little girl be-ing immediately charmed by Jase's impeccable man-ners and savoir faire. Jase had been astonishingly handsome, too, with perfect features, thick, graying hair and a youthful, well-cared-for body. He had dressed with remarkably good taste. He had done ev-erything with good taste, Tracy had learned when Jase began asking her out.

He had never rushed her. For months he'd escorted her to the very finest restaurants, to the theater, to the ballet, to lectures. He had always had consideration and concern for her likes and dislikes. She'd realized she was falling in love with him long before he'd even attempted to kiss her, and when it had finally happened, she'd been overwhelmed and gratified to discover she also had a strong sexual desire for this man she was already in love with.

From that moment their relationship had changed. She'd discovered that Jase was an extremely sensual man. During the months they'd planned their wedding he'd taught her the joys of making love, at first utterly amazed that she had been a virgin.

Jase had made her happy, Tracy admitted with a sad sigh. She seldom let herself dwell on the past, for the wonderful memories never failed to make her sad. But tonight she couldn't help her thoughts. Perhaps deviating from her normal behavior in such a shocking manner was enough to make her dig into her past for some sort of lifeline.

Jase's sudden death, caused by a massive heart attack, had completely debilitated Tracy for a period. Then the attorneys and accountants had shocked her out of her numbness. She had had a financial empire on her hands, and that was something she hadn't been prepared for. While they had lived very well, she had never had an inkling of the size and complexity of Jase's fortune. Her father had been a big help. He'd not only understood her grief, having faced the same trauma years before when Tracy's mother had died, but had given Tracy invaluable financial advice whenever she'd asked. In the long run, though, it was Tracy who'd had to get hold of herself and take over.

That was what she'd been doing for the past year, turning herself into quite a different woman from the polished, carefree wife of a successful man she'd been during her four-year marriage. This trip had been the culmination of a growing interest in Jase's estate, a genuine interest. To her intense satisfaction, Tracy realized she had quite a flair for business, and with the assistance of some very able people she was handling the properties she'd inherited very well.

But now there was the Double J. And Slade Dawson. Tracy knew instinctively that there was something wrong here. And not just from the scene on the balcony, though there was no question that that had been a dire mistake. But beyond that, starting with Slade's completely uncalled-for antagonism at her arrival and encompassing Rachel's quixotic behavior, something was definitely amiss. But what?

She would work on finding the answer. Slade couldn't hide in ''town'' all the time. Yes, tonight was going to make dealing with him more difficult, but she had no choice in the matter. The only way she could finish up here quickly was to spend time with him.

With a moan, Tracy turned over onto her stomach and pulled the pillow over her head. How on earth was she even going to face the man, let alone conduct business with him? What must he think of her? All he'd done was touch her, and she'd melted into a pool of passion.

And there was no denying that she still felt it.

Tracy rolled over again. She had to maintain some decorum, she simply had to. She had been so humiliatingly willing. And it really was Slade who had backed off.

How very odd for a man to make such erotic overtures and suddenly back off, she thought. He'd been concerned about something, and she was sure there was a reason for the strange expression he'd worn at that particular moment. Did it have the same foundation as his original antagonism?

Sleep was a long time coming.

Three

————

"Gone? Gone where?" Tracy exclaimed in confusion.

Tracy had slept until eight, then spent an hour bathing and getting dressed. Wearing designer jeans, a trim white blouse and high-heeled boots, and with her hair and makeup flawless, she was ready to inspect the ranch. But Rachel had just told her Slade was gone, and the woman looked as if she thought she had just done Tracy a tremendous service.

Maybe she had. The prospect of seeing Slade this morning wasn't exactly pleasant. Yet she hadn't expected him to leave the ranch again.

Rachel never stopped bustling around the kitchen, intent on getting Tracy some breakfast. "He went up to Big Bluff. He left a note. It's over there on the table."

"I see." Frowning, Tracy crossed the room. The "note" was just a small slip of paper folded in two, and she straightened it and read quickly: Rachel. Went to Big Bluff for a few days. Slade.

"What's Big Bluff?" Tracy asked, oddly upset by this turn of events. She should have been grateful Slade had made himself scarce. Instead, a very suspect disappointment churned within her.

"It's a mountain. Slade's got a hunting cabin up there. He goes off by himself every once in a while."

Tracy's frown remained set. "I would think he might have waited until we had a chance to talk. Ben can show me the ranch—that's no problem—but I did want to speak to Slade about a few matters."

Rachel looked surprised. "Well, now, that's too bad. Perhaps Ben or I might be able to answer them." Rachel gestured toward the coffeepot. "Would you like some coffee?"

"Yes, thank you." While the housekeeper filled two mugs, Tracy sat at the table. "I do have questions, Rachel. A few have arisen since I got here," she said pointedly, detecting an immediate wariness in Rachel's expression.

"I only meant questions about the ranch," Rachel said hastily. "Anything else you'll just have to ask Slade about."

"He's made that rather difficult to do." Tracy took a sip of coffee and set the mug down. "You knew my husband, didn't you?"

Rachel's face immediately closed up. Tracy expected the woman to be loyal to Slade, but she felt that if she steered clear of his name, if all she did was ask a few questions about Jase's connection with the Double J, there shouldn't be a problem. "I guess what I'm curious about is how Jase ever got involved with a ranch," she confessed. Rachel just looked even more tight-lipped.

Tracy tried again. "Did Jase come to the ranch often? He took a lot of business trips, but he was always vague about where he was going. Since his death, I've learned…" Her voice trailed off. She was talking to a deaf woman. Rachel was more than wary now; she was looking trapped. "Rachel, what's wrong?"

The woman's lips were thin. "You'll have to get your information from Slade, Tracy. It's not my place to talk about those things."

"What things?" Her questions had been so basic, just simple inquiries about Jase's possible visits to the ranch. Why would they put Rachel on the defensive?

Rachel's voice was guarded, almost sullen. "Things about…your husband. I'm not a gossip."

"Well, of course you're not!" Aghast, Tracy got up. "I really don't understand, Rachel, but please forgive me if I gave you the wrong impression. I didn't realize I was stepping out-of-bounds." The apology was sincere, even if Tracy saw no reason for it. What had she asked that was so terrible?

Picking up her mug, Tracy started for the door.

"Please don't fix those eggs now. I'll eat something later. I think I'd like to take a little walk."

"Tracy!"

There was a plea in Rachel's voice, and Tracy stopped at the door and turned.

"I'm sorry," Rachel said. "I know I sounded rude. But you really will have to talk to Slade if you want some answers. It's his business, not mine."

Tracy nodded thoughtfully. "I may have to do that, even though he's doing his best to make it impossible. I'll see you in a little while, Rachel."

Later in the day, Ben cheerfully acted as tour guide for her. Tracy tried to show interest in the barns, the tack room and the corrals, but it was all pretense until Ben stopped at the horse pasture. "These Thoroughbreds are Slade's pride and joy," he told her.

"They're beautiful animals," Tracy was able to say with the first real enthusiasm of the afternoon. Ever since her strange and upsetting conversation with Rachel, Tracy's mind hadn't been on the ranch. There seemed to be a strange whirlpool of confusion in her brain. Thoughts of Jase and Slade went around and around, disconnected, then connected, whirling amid a montage of unanswered questions.

Ben seemed blissfully unaware of her preoccupation. "Do you ride?"

"I used to, years ago."

"Well, now, how about me saddling a couple of horses and taking a little ride? You could see some of the pastures and cattle that way."

She agreed immediately. She'd been so preoccupied for the last twenty-four hours that the thought of riding through open fields was indeed refreshing. Maybe the ride would make her shake this strange mood, though she suspected nothing other than some straightforward answers would satisfy what was becoming a burning curiosity.

Feeling as if she'd been given a royal runaround on the Double J, she waited in the shade of the barn while Ben saddled the horses. She pondered Rachel's strange innuendos. What was it Slade could tell her about Jase? What an odd answer Rachel had given her, and to such a simple question. Why had the older woman made a big deal out of how many times Jase had come to the ranch?

Whatever the reason for the mystery, she'd never know about it unless she saw Slade again. This meant waiting until he decided to come back. There was something almost eerie about the whole thing, starting with Slade's inexplicable anger at her unannounced arrival. Now she suspected his rudeness hadn't come from mere grouchiness. He really had been upset. But why? And was that the reason he kept trying to avoid her, just so she couldn't question him?

And what about last night? He hadn't seemed to want to avoid her on the balcony. But he'd stopped in time. What if it had all been up to her...?

Tracy felt a tight band clamp around her chest. Why had she ever let Slade Dawson kiss her? Worse, why had she kissed him back?

Ben led a small gray mare over to her. "This is

Dolly." He grinned. "She's a good old girl and won't give you a bit of trouble."

"Thank you."

Tracy put her foot in the stirrup and swung up into the saddle, reaching down to pat the mare's neck once she was securely seated. "She's a nice horse, Ben."

Ben mounted a big chestnut, and they walked the horses through the yard to a gate in the fenceline. Once they were on the other side, with the gate latched behind them again, Ben asked, "How long are you staying in Montana, Tracy?"

They rode side by side in an enormous field of grass liberally sprinkled with blue and yellow wildflowers. "I had planned to leave in the morning," Tracy replied, keeping her face impassive. "Now I'm not sure."

"If you're going to be here a few more days, we could plan a longer ride if you'd like, up into the mountains, maybe," Ben said pleasantly.

"The mountains?" Tracy's heart did a broad jump, and she eyed Ben, suddenly realizing he might not be quite so reticent as his sister. "Where's Big Bluff, Ben?"

"Big Bluff is about ten miles that way," he answered without curiosity, nodding toward the west. "Slade's got a hunting cabin up there. Rachel said this morning he went up there for a few days. He does that every so often."

"Just to get away by himself?" she questioned softly. She knew that pumping Ben was dirty pool, but she didn't care. Something was odd on the Double

J, out of kilter, and it involved Jase, and Slade and, though she couldn't imagine how, herself. She had every right to know what it was.

Ben shrugged. "Guess so. Slade's kind of an odd duck, a loner. He's an all-right guy. Just likes to be left alone."

"Yes, I gathered that," she returned dryly, realizing she was developing quite a curiosity about Slade Dawson. Rachel's odd remarks had only whetted that curiosity. "Has he always lived on the Double J?"

"Yup. Born here, and lived right here all his life. Well, maybe that's not a hundred percent true. Slade was in the marines for a while, then he was off at some school for a couple of years. But other than that he's been right here."

"I see." Tracy smiled faintly. The smile didn't quite reach her green eyes. "Do you run off to Big Bluff sometimes, too, Ben?"

Ben laughed easily. "Once in a while. It's a beautiful spot and sort of heals you up, if you know what I mean."

Tracy nodded. Ben's casual comment raised some interesting possibilities. Had Slade been emotionally bruised by the balcony episode? He hadn't shown it. But then, what had he shown? Actually, once she had come to her senses, he'd only wanted to get away from her. Yes, she could remember that quite clearly now.

Mentally she railed at herself. How could she have been so weak last night? Well, Slade Dawson would never have another opportunity to put his hands on her, even if she decided to wait and confront him.

The thought gave birth to a question, and she turned to Ben. "How long would it take to ride to Big Bluff, Ben?"

He looked surprised. "You want to go up there?"

"There are some things I should talk to Slade about before I leave. I didn't expect him to go off like this without any warning."

Ben pulled his hat off, smoothed his hair down and settled the Stetson back on his head before answering. "Well, it doesn't take all that long, I guess."

"But you're not really thrilled about going," Tracy added, reading Ben's reluctance accurately. "Could I find it alone?"

"You? Hell, no. You'd get lost in those mountains, Tracy. There are a hundred trails running every which way."

"Couldn't you draw me a map?"

He stared at her. "You're bent on going?"

"It's either that or wait until he comes down. How long do you think he'll be?"

"Rachel said a few days. That might be best, Tracy. Just hang around until he gets back. He probably wouldn't like us barging in on him, anyway."

"Wouldn't he? Well, I'll tell you something, Ben, I'm just a little tired of everyone worrying about what Slade wouldn't like. To hell with him! I own this ranch, too!"

Red-faced, Tracy apologized immediately. "I'm sorry, Ben. I shouldn't take my anger at Slade out on you. It's just that I've never met anyone quite like him before. Maybe I'm not handling it well.'' That was almost comic understatement, Tracy realized with a jab of very real dislike. Lashing out at Ben when she was really irritated with Slade was upsetting.

''Forget it. Sometimes Slade makes me mad as hell, too.'' Ben grinned boyishly and the sun-bronzed skin around his eyes crinkled. ''Slade isn't easy to get to know.''

''Easy? More like impossible!''

Ben laughed congenially. ''Yeah, I guess so. Actually, he's one of those people who don't make friends easily, but when they do, it's a real solid friendship. Know the type?''

''The strong silent type?'' Tracy drawled sarcastically.

''Like in the movies? Naw, Slade's not like that. He's strong and silent, I guess, but he's no phony. He's not one of them Fancy Dans who've never been near a horse or a working ranch. There isn't one job here that Slade can't do better than any of the hands. He's the best at everything, riding, roping. Hell, he's won all kinds of rodeo awards.''

Tracy listened, tense. She was still curious and was soaking up Ben's words. She also harbored resentment. Everyone on the Double J admitted Slade's bad humor, but was quick to point out how completely wonderful he was at the same time. The best at everything, indeed! How ridiculous.

Nudging Dolly into a canter, Tracy pulled ahead.

"Go to the right," Ben called. "There's a spring, and the horses can have a drink."

They dismounted and walked around while the horses dipped into the clear, cool water. Tracy bent to pick a wildflower. "You know, Ben, I came here thinking this was just going to be a routine visit." With a frustrated sigh, Tracy examined the small blue flower in her hand. "I have a feeling nothing is simply 'routine' with Slade Dawson. And there's something else, too, something Rachel said to ask Slade about. It's made me very uneasy. Am I letting my imagination get carried away?"

Ben looked off to the mountainous horizon with a reflective squint. "Tracy, there are things—well, there are some pretty unusual factors...."

"Yes?" she prompted.

He looked at her intently. "It doesn't have anything to do with you and probably would only hurt. Don't ask. For your own sake, stay the hell out of it."

She felt Ben had intended to say a lot more but had changed his mind. With a dejected glance around the pasture at the grazing cattle, Tracy went to Dolly and picked up the trailing reins. "Let's go back, Ben. I've seen enough for today."

Tracy slept like the dead that night and awoke feeling as though she hadn't so much as moved a muscle for nine hours. Through the open French doors, she could see a few fleecy clouds in the blue morning sky, and she watched their lazy, barely perceptible movements with an unusual feeling of serenity. Amazing what a good night's sleep will do, she reflected.

Maybe now, with her mind clear and some time elapsed, she could see everything that had happened since her arrival with a keener eye. It was certain that Slade's surliness had thrown her off balance right from the outset, and Rachel's apparent distress when she'd heard her name had been confusing, too.

The unsettling incident when Tracy had arrived stayed in her mind, giving rise to a dozen questions. She also couldn't understand Rachel's refusal to discuss Jase in the most innocent fashion, or Ben's suggestion that she forget the whole thing. Forget what?

She'd hoped Jase's peculiar involvement with a ranch would make some sort of sense after she'd taken a look at the Double J, but instead the whole thing was turning into a rather irritating mystery. Then, of course, there was the incident with Slade....

Tracy closed her eyes, blocking out the sunlight, and immediately and easily transported herself back in time. How odd that she could remember every tiny detail of those intimate minutes in Slade Dawson's arms. What was she going to do, retain the memory against her better judgment? Why dwell on something that should never have happened? Surely she wasn't genuinely attracted to that ill-mannered lout?

In the clear light of day, it was quite easy to wonder what had possessed her. There was only one conclusion she could reach about the whole thing: she had to make sure it didn't happen again.

Slade Dawson's actions seemed to have been caused by his shock at her suddenly showing up at the Double J, and by a second shock when he'd opened the bathroom door. Perhaps those were reasons enough for his initial disappearance. Nothing explained what had happened on the balcony, however, though it had apparently prompted Slade's flight to the mountains.

Still, she found that reasoning hard to believe. Slade was a grown man, certainly able to face a woman the morning after a chance encounter, even if he thought it had been a mistake. No, Tracy had a strong feeling that whatever had prodded Slade to leave was the same thing Rachel wouldn't talk about, the same thing Ben had warned her against. Something that touched on Jase. It didn't seem possible, but somehow Jase was at the core of what was going on.

What bothered Tracy most was that this hinted at yet another facet of a husband who, as she'd been discovering for a year, she hadn't known as well as she'd thought.

It had stunned her that Jase had kept so much about his business to himself, and it had made her realize she had shared only one portion of his life. Beyond their beautiful home life, Jase's activities had been shrouded in secrecy. She didn't understand why, however, because since taking over the estate she had discovered nothing he couldn't have spoken openly of to anyone.

Until now.

Tracy's heart did a flip. What could there be about the Double J to have made Jase so secretive? It made more sense to attribute his reticence merely to an innate need for privacy.

Tracy realized she had to make a decision about whether to wait until Slade got back or to call Brock McFee and arrange a departure time. The one thing that bothered her about picking up and leaving the Double J without answers was her ingrained compulsion to tie up loose ends. If she returned to San Francisco at this point, she would forever wonder what she hadn't taken the time to uncover.

And if she stayed she would have to make some phone calls, to her father and to her office.

Tracy made up her mind. She would stay, and to heck with what Slade might make of her still being at the ranch when he finally came back. With that firmly in mind, Tracy threw back the covers and got up.

In the bathroom, she made sure the lock caught, having learned the hard way that the ancient contraption didn't always work. Not that anyone was apt to walk in on her today. With Slade away, the only threat on the Double J was effectively eliminated.

Catching her mirrored reflection, Tracy had to admit the truth in that conjecture. Slade was a threat in more ways than one. But he would find out, if he tried another personal advance, that she could be a threat, too. She owned half this ranch, a share equal to his. If he pushed her too hard, he just might find his management position questioned. That, from what Tracy had been able to detect, was something that had been left strictly alone. In fact, records on the Double J consisted merely of facts and figures on financial statements, with not one single comment on the quality of the ranch's management.

Well, that just might be her ace in the hole in dealing with the likes of Slade Dawson. While she certainly hadn't spotted any blatant neglect or oversights in the ranch's operation, she was in a position to make things hot for Slade if she chose. She wouldn't hesitate to remind him of that should it become necessary.

The range of mountains stretched as far north as the eye could see, curving around the southern rim of the valley. They didn't look as menacing as Ben had declared them to be, thought Tracy as she urged Dolly slowly forward. Rather, they looked like sleeping giants, a towering framework of rich colors for the lush valley below, certainly nothing to evoke terror in one's heart. Not even a city-born heart.

It was unnerving to imagine Slade behind one of those craggy peaks or secreted in a shadowy crevice, maybe watching her with field glasses.

It wasn't all that likely, really, but if he was watching, he must be terribly disappointed that she hadn't left. A small, vengeful feeling of glee accompanied the thought, along with a sense of justification for wanting vengeance. She'd already cooled her heels for three days, and she still had no hint of when Slade might return. It was hard not to think of Slade Dawson without hoping he was suffering.

Not that she hadn't enjoyed the three days. She had, surprisingly enough. The Double J was a beautiful place, a retreat almost, peaceful, quiet, unhurried. It offered a way of life that was growing increasingly appealing to Tracy.

Rachel had been very nice about her extended stay, accepting the uncomplicated explanation that she needed a few more days' rest after her arduous travels. It really wasn't a lie, it just wasn't the whole truth.

But after days of idle relaxation, Tracy could sense the housekeeper's and Ben's curiosity. They were both beginning to understand that she was really waiting for Slade, and a few times Tracy had caught a troubled light in their eyes.

The freedom to ride Dolly alone had been won only after Ben's assurances that Tracy could handle a horse. She'd received a long lecture about not wandering far, getting back fast should a storm come up, watching for snakes and on and on. To Tracy's amusement, Rachel's warnings had encompassed every danger known to man and then some.

"I'll be very careful," she'd promised, accepting Rachel's maternal nature without rancor. During Slade's absence, Tracy had grown very fond of the older woman, maintaining a comfortable relationship by staying away from controversial subjects.

A gate in the fence, unnoticed until she was right beside it, looked interesting. Just beyond the barbed wire, boulders and large rocks marked the demarcation line between flat pastureland and rolling hills. Beyond the grassy hills, Tracy could see the dark green of heavily timbered mountains. She was positive this was the spot that Ben had indicated when she'd asked him where Big Bluff was located. So through that fence and upward along the trail she could see winding around the hillside, now visible, now lost behind a curve or boulder, was Slade.

With directions or a map, she knew she could find him. If he didn't return soon, she planned to give it a try. She couldn't wait indefinitely, and if she had to risk getting lost in the wilds of Montana, she would. That shouldn't be a problem, however. There were a half-dozen men working on the Double J besides Ben and Slade. It would be a simple and unsuspicious task to engage one of them in conversation and get the information she needed.

How much longer should she give him? With a reflective frown, Tracy turned Dolly's head and began the ride back. As horse and rider approached grazing cattle, the white-faced, reddish-brown animals chewed in their incessant, rhythmic way.

Tracy knew she was seeing the Double J at its very best. Winter had to alter the scenic wonder of the valley, had to make life harsher, more difficult. Yet even blanketed with snow the fields would be lovely. The landscape would be changed, but it would still have a stark beauty all its own.

She would like to see it with snow on the ground, under the pale sky of winter, she realized, marveling that only a few days on the ranch had reshaped the rather blasé attitude she had arrived with. But how would Slade take another visit?

Tracy smirked at the answer she came up with: he'd probably run for Big Bluff again.

Dolly nickered softly, and Tracy saw why. They were near the spring, and the little mare had caught the scent of water. Smiling, Tracy relaxed her hold on the reins, allowing Dolly to approach the small, crystal-clear pool. She slid to the ground and patted the mare's neck. "Have your drink," she said as she dismounted.

With a sigh, Tracy walked around the spring, then sank to the grass, adjusting her position so that she could see the trail into the hills. Absently she plucked grassy stalks, her thoughts on Slade again.

He was a stranger, a man she hadn't exchanged more than a few words with, and they had been bitter words. Yet those moments on the balcony overshadowed all others in her past. It made little sense, there was no logic for it, but it was true. She had a memory she couldn't ignore. She would take it back to San Francisco with her. And when she saw Slade again she would think of it.

But that wasn't why she stayed, she told herself with determined vehemence. The moment she learned whatever it was everyone was so secretive about, she would leave. And it was silly contemplating a return visit next winter. That was something she would put out of her mind completely. Memories were something she couldn't erase, but she could prevent storing up any more.

All she wanted to do was learn about Jase. She had a right to know his secrets about the ranch. Then it would be "goodbye" to the Double J. Forever.

Four

Slade managed to stay busy at the cabin. Any time spent at Big Bluff during temperate weather meant chopping wood and working on the stockpile so that there would be heat during his wintertime visits. He threw himself into the chore energetically, varying the routine with general maintenance in and around the cabin. The projects were supposed to keep him therapeutically occupied.

It was disturbing to realize that no amount of physical exhaustion could keep Tracy Moorland out of his thoughts. He could fall into bed bone-weary, but the moment he relaxed, there she was. Her image haunted him.

Slade knew he wasn't a man whose head was easily turned by a pretty face. At the moment, however, he was questioning several bothersome traits he seemed to have picked up recently. For one, it wasn't just Tracy's looks that gnawed at him. She had come to mean too much to him. It was ridiculous. Yet he knew as surely as grass was green that if she were anyone but a Moorland he would pursue her.

The Moorland name. That was the bind. While it had had an almost infamous effect on his past, it had remained tenuous, intangible. Now it had come to life; it had substance, and it was intolerable coming in the form of a beautiful, sensual woman. For the first time in his thirty-two years he'd had to face a Moorland, and just because it wasn't old Jason himself, that didn't lessen the pain.

On top of that, his beer-influenced desire for vengeance in Shorty's Bar and his stupidity on the balcony were both so disgusting that he could barely stand thinking about them. All he could do was thank God that he hadn't let a crazy passion for a woman he had no right to carry him beyond the point of no return.

On the fifth day of his self-imposed exile, Slade awoke to heavy gray clouds and the realization that he had no supplies left. He had to go back, whether he wanted to or not. Needing to put off his return until the last possible moment, and actually praying Tracy Moorland would be gone, he delayed starting the ride until noon. Then he saddled Poncho, his horse, secured his gear and climbed aboard. It was either go back or go without food.

* * *

Tracy had seen many summer storms, but nothing to compare with the wild display of sheet lightning and explosive thunder besieging the valley that afternoon. She stood at the kitchen window and watched the changing light, the brilliant flashes, the ominous, ever-darkening sky. "It'll rain before night," Rachel predicted confidently.

"I hope it does," Tracy proclaimed, feeling very unsettled in the tense, prestorm atmosphere.

Rachel stopped behind her and peered out the same window. "It's already raining in the mountains," she remarked, and unconcernedly returned to the chicken she was frying.

"Oh?" The mountains remained a distant challenge. Ben's invitation to "take a ride in the mountains" should she stay around long enough had been neatly sidestepped, and Tracy's decision to explore on her own hadn't quite reached fruition. Maybe she'd go tomorrow, she silently mused, if the weather permitted. A storm might preclude a lot of things. "What about Slade?" she asked quietly.

Rachel laughed. "He's not made of sugar. He won't melt."

Tracy smiled in spite of herself, agreeing silently that Slade Dawson wasn't even remotely sugary. She kept an eye on the threatening sky. "It really is getting bad," she said softly.

"Are you worried about Slade?" Rachel asked, amazed.

"No, of course not. But—"

Rachel's hands went to her hips. "Now why would

you be worried about him? You know, I have the strangest feeling..." Rachel looked more concerned than amused, although Tracy could have sworn she was teasing her. Then the older woman sighed and added, "I guess you wouldn't be the first female he's riled who found herself worrying about him."

"Oh?" Tracy's eyebrows shot up. "Is Slade a ladies' man? I really didn't get that impression." Nor did she want to get it now, she realized with a strange, unfathomable feeling of weakness.

"He gets his share," Rachel remarked dryly, concentrating once again on the sizzling chicken.

Something recoiled within Tracy as Rachel's earthy comment evoked a parade of faceless women. Was that all the kiss on the balcony had been about, merely an opportunity seized? They'd been alone on a beautiful, romantic night, a woman and a man in an unexpected communion. Perhaps what had happened was something Slade was so used to that it didn't even warrant his attention. Maybe he didn't even remember.

How unfair, if that was the case. Why should he be able to put it aside when she couldn't? In the past year, Tracy hadn't even thought of a relationship with another man. But if she had, she realized, she would want it to encompass the wild, incredible passion of Slade's embrace.

Her thoughts wandered, leaping beyond the window and meshing with the gathering storm. The most incredible possibility occurred to her. Surely all her reasons for wanting to see Slade weren't merely contrived excuses to cover a simple desire to experience his magnetism again?

"Hah!" she muttered.

"Beg your pardon?"

"Nothing, Rachel." Tracy headed for the door. "I'm going for a walk."

"In this?" Rachel shook her head. "Don't go too far. When it does start raining, it'll be a downpour."

Tracy dashed out the door, promising to stay close to the house. A wind was coming up, and crossing the backyard she bucked its growing force, her hair whipping around her face. Her casual yellow dress was molded to her body, but she didn't turn back.

She had no destination in mind, just a restless need to get out of the house for a few minutes. But automatically she headed for the Thoroughbreds' pasture, a route that took her very close to the horse barn.

She didn't see Slade, but he saw her and cursed loudly and efficiently. Dammit, she was still here. Damn!

Slade watched her with a crazy mixture of feelings from the tack room window. She was even more beautiful than he remembered. She was also a nightmarish problem. What in hell was he going to do about Tracy Moorland? It was certain he wasn't unaffected by her. But he had a lot more to worry about than this woman's sex appeal.

His eyes narrowed as he wondered what Rachel might have told her. He rubbed the heavy whisker stubble on his jaw, trying to decide whether Tracy would still be around if she knew the truth. Somehow he doubted it. So if his hunch was right, she still didn't know who he was.

But why hadn't she gone home as she'd planned? Was she waiting to see him again?

An immediate flame sparked in his loins, an invisible cord stretching from her to him, winding around his vitals. Had that kiss been so memorable that she wanted an encore? He couldn't doubt it; it had ravaged his brain, too. But good Lord, it had only been a kiss.

That wasn't exactly accurate. Not when those long, shapely legs had curled around his hips and he had tasted the sweet honey of the most perfect breasts he'd ever seen.

Dammit! he thought. Nothing had changed. Not one blasted thing. The thought that the situation was exactly as it had been when he'd slipped away that morning was maddening. He'd wasted his time. He was back at square one.

Even if leaving had solved nothing, at least Big Bluff had been peaceful. Maybe he should just get some more supplies and go back.

No, he couldn't. He had work to do.

Grunting in disgust at the whole situation, Slade walked from the tack room to the barn, striding back to where he'd left Poncho. Quickly he wiped the horse down and filled his feed box with hay, and after gathering up the canvas clothes bag and the now-empty food pack he left the barn. The wind was strong enough that he had trouble closing the doors with his arms full. A voice behind him—one that didn't surprise him—drawled, "Well, well, the prodigal returns."

He shot Tracy a hard glance, ignoring the impression of cold green eyes and billowing hair, of curves too sweet to be believed. "Don't start anything," he warned.

Tracy's mouth dropped open. How dare he be defensive? *She* was the injured party here. At the very least he could have the decency to look a little apologetic for wasting nearly a week of her time. But there certainly wasn't an apology lurking among his dark whiskers and steely gray eyes. The man was impossible. What was that damnably stupid idea she'd had about his magnetism?

"Why ever would I start anything?" she returned. "Just because I've been stuck here for five days waiting for you? My goodness, how small of me to be upset over such a trivial matter."

"Can the sarcasm." Irritated that one of the doors wouldn't catch properly, Slade tossed the things he'd been carrying to the ground and gave his full attention to the door.

"No sarcasm? How about fury? Can you deal with fury? Or murder? I could easily murder you right now." It was hard to be stiff with anger in this wind, but Tracy was giving it her best shot. And it wasn't pretense. She *was* angry, and while she hadn't planned a frontal attack at Slade's return, she also hadn't planned on him being so fractious.

Slade gave her another hard look. "What've you got to be furious about? You wanted what you got."

The kiss! The *bastard* was actually referring to that night on the balcony and insinuating that she had asked for it! Well, he'd never know it hurt, not if she had to Superglue a smile to her face! "Oh, that," she said disdainfully, as if the time in his arms had long been forgotten. "That's not what I could murder you over."

"It's not?"

Aha! She silently exulted. Success. He looked puzzled. Taken aback. Now to solidify his perplexity. "Of course not. Why would you think that? But your running off to play Daniel Boone when you knew full well I'd come here to inspect the ranch, that's another matter. I'm not exactly thrilled at having had to hang around until you got tired of mountain climbing or chasing bears or whatever the heck you did for five days."

"Why did you have to hang around? You could have inspected the ranch without me."

By this time they were practically shouting, not from emotion but to be heard above the wind. "We'll talk about it later," Tracy yelled.

"What?" A flash of lightning, followed by a clap of thunder, rocked the air and the sky opened up, releasing a deluge of raindrops as big as dimes. Slade pulled the barn door open again. "Get inside," he yelled. Tracy ran past him, and he gathered up his gear and quickly followed, securing the door behind them. "What the hell are you wandering around in a storm for?" he snapped.

Tracy gave her head a toss to settle her tangled hair.

"It wasn't this bad when I left the house," she answered sharply, flapping the fabric of her skirt to shake some raindrops from it.

"But it's been obvious for the last hour what was coming," Slade persisted.

"Is that what finally brought you out of hiding?" she taunted.

"I wasn't hiding!"

"Of course you were hiding. Don't take me for a fool, Slade. I might be a lot of things, but a fool isn't one of them." Not all the time, she added mentally. The rain pummeling the metal roof of the barn sounded like a thousand drums. Tracy looked up and frowned.

"That's hail!" Slade exclaimed, and opened the door a crack. "Wow," he said softly.

"Let me see!" Eager to witness the hail for herself, Tracy peeked past him. "Oh, my goodness!" Marble-sized hailstones were hitting the ground with such force that they were bouncing several times before settling, creating a remarkably turbulent scene. "I've never seen hail that big before," she said, amazed.

Slade felt her leaning forward, her thigh brushing his, her hand on his arm, her scent a fragrant teaser. He knew that if he didn't move away immediately he'd repeat what he was already sorry for and would be even sorrier for should it happen again. Abruptly he closed the door and leaned against it, his eyes hooded, unrevealing. "We'll have to wait here till the hail stops. Shouldn't be long."

Why did everything suddenly seem more intimate?

Tracy thought. And much too warm, airless. Tracy moved away from Slade's menacing form. "Can you open the door again, just a crack? It's too...close in here."

He only stared, taking in the red stain on her cheeks, the excited but fearful look in her eyes. Damn, this would never do, he thought. Too much had happened between them for them to be alone like this. She was thinking of it, just as he was, and though she could act as relaxed as she wanted to about that night, she hadn't been able to forget it, either. That was why she was still here.

It was painful to realize she wouldn't push him away if he reached for her. They could climb the ladder to the second story and finish what they'd started on the balcony, make love with the sweet smell of alfalfa hay beneath them and the sound of the hail crashing on the roof.

Slade shook his head, chasing away the foolish thoughts. He moved away from the door. Hail never fell for long, thank God. It should only be a few minutes before he could break this up. He worked at calming himself. She was still here, still in the dark about who he was. All he could do was make the best of a bad situation.

He leaned against a workbench. "Did you look around the ranch?"

Tracy was astonished. Was he actually going to act like a normal human being? She searched the craggy lines of his face and saw a strange control.

She had bided her time for five days, waiting for a

chance to talk. All right, she'd give him the benefit of the doubt and forget the past few minutes. "Yes. Ben very kindly showed me around."

"Then why—"

"Why am I still here? Because I need to talk to you. Both Ben and Rachel refuse to discuss Jase, and—"

Slade's expression turned grim. "And you think I will?"

"Is there any good reason not to?"

"There's nothing to discuss," he stated coolly.

Tracy's eyes widened in genuine perplexity. "You mean to stand there and tell me you won't answer a few simple questions about Jase? Why not?"

Slade's mind worked feverishly. He wanted to throw her off the scent. What kind of information had she been trying to get out of Rachel and Ben? "What questions?" he asked softly.

Tracy heaved a somewhat relieved sigh. Maybe he was going to cooperate, "After Jase died and I took over the estate, I was very surprised to see a ranch among his holdings. You see, everything else he left is urban property. Another point that makes the Double J unique is the partnership. Jase had one hundred percent ownership in every other property. I'm sure you can see from those things alone that I arrived here with a certain amount of curiosity."

He hadn't asked for her life story, but Slade listened without comment. In fact, he enjoyed the expression on her face and the intelligence in her green eyes as she spoke. But the content of her words was disturbing. Slade knew what she was leading up to and wondered how to handle it. He was surprised when, for no apparent reason, she became somewhat embarrassed.

"You see, Jase never talked about business with me, and I was quite in the dark."

Slade tuned the rest of what sounded like a personal confession out, pondering the part about Jason Moorland keeping things from his wife. Obviously he had kept everything to himself, not just business. That explained why Tracy didn't know who Slade Dawson really was.

His gaze washed over the yellow dress in a slow scrutiny that Tracy wasn't even aware of as she talked. If she hadn't been so wrapped up in her story, however, she would have seen the knowing light in Slade's eyes and maybe even have sensed the erotic nature of his thoughts.

But Slade's facial expression didn't change, not even when his gaze lingered on the swells of her breasts.

"So you see," Tracy said, "I can't help having a few questions, like how you and Jase ever became partners, and how often he came to the ranch and—"

Straightening from a deceptively casual slouch, Slade said, "He never came to the ranch."

Tracy frowned. "Never?"

"Never."

"I don't understand."

Slade shrugged. "I can't help that. You asked a question, I gave you an answer."

"But the partnership. How? Why?"

A lie was due about now. Shifting his weight, Slade plunged into it. "I don't know why your husband bought the Double J. It was before my time. I never met the man." Only part of that statement was a lie, he realized wryly as he listened to his own words.

Tracy tried to put it all together. There were too many discrepancies in Slade's simplistic reply. She was positive, although Rachel hadn't admitted it, that the woman had met Jase. Had it been before Slade was born? Had Jase been involved with the ranch that long? Still, none of this explained Rachel's and Ben's reluctance to talk about the past.

Uneasy, not sure she'd learned anything of any importance, Tracy turned away, her arms folded in front of her. She stopped at the window. "It's rain now," she murmured.

Slade came to life. Drawing a harsh breath, he pulled his denim jacket from the clothes bag. "Here, put this over your head and make a run for it," he commanded gruffly.

"All right." Tracy draped the jacket over her shoulders. "We can talk again later," she said, hearing an unsettled tremor in her own voice.

"There's nothing more to talk about," he snapped.

Tracy froze. "Maybe what you should have said was, you don't intend talking about it further. If there's nothing more, why did Rachel tell me to ask you about it? She could have told me as much as you just did."

Slade looked away, his heart beating hard. His only

refuge was anger. "Keep out of something that's none of your business," he growled.

Astounded, Tracy watched Slade's extreme discomfort. He was much too upset for her not to be suspicious. Like Rachel, he was making too much out of nothing. Tracy's gaze roamed curiously. His jaw was dark with whiskers, attesting to little concern with his appearance during his absence. He still radiated the magnetism she'd tried to ignore. What was there about this man that reached beneath her skin and touched her very core?

At this moment, whiskers and all, she wouldn't push him away should he make a personal overture...and she could hardly believe it. Had she lost every ounce of her ordinary common sense? Rudeness was something that had always turned her off. Yet the ruder Slade Dawson was, the more attracted to him she became. She felt a deep-seated concern over the dark emotions he so effortlessly brought to life.

She felt at a loss as to how to deal with them and with Slade. She could throw her financial weight around and cause trouble, but trouble was something she preferred avoiding whenever possible. How much better it would be if she could shape their bewildering relationship into something palatable. She should at least try.

Her eyes registered a trace of wistfulness. "Slade, we got off to a bad start. I don't know why, but we did. I'm willing to shake hands and start over. We're partners here, and I'd like to be able to discuss the ranch with you on an intelligent, businesslike basis. Your plans, for instance. I'm sure you must have ideas about the Double J's future.''

Slade's eyes narrowed. What was she pulling now? Warily he nodded. ''I have plans.''

''With the Thoroughbreds?''

Out of all the facets of the operation she'd seen, she had picked out the one closest to his heart. It amazed Slade that she could be so perceptive. The only reason the ranch didn't already boast a track and a special training area for the Thoroughbreds was lack of money. The Double J was moderately profitable, but not profitable enough for expensive improvements. And Slade would never mortgage the land for anything. The land was inviolable, too valuable to risk, even for the longtime hope of someday expanding the horse-breeding phase of the operation.

But he wasn't ready to share his dream, not with a woman he didn't trust. A Moorland. ''I have a few ideas'' was all he allowed.

Tracy released a pent-up breath. ''I was sure you did. The place reflects your good care, Slade, and I was sure you must have a lot of plans in mind. The Thoroughbreds—''

''Are none of your concern,'' Slade put in harshly. ''Look, do you have a problem with the way I've been running the ranch? If you do, just say so. Let's get it out in the open.''

His rebuff hurt. She had offered friendship and he had turned it down. Tracy's chin came up. ''Why are you so defensive? What are you trying so hard to keep hidden, Slade?''

''This conversation is over,'' Slade stated coldly. ''The hail's stopped. Go on up to the house.''

''I'll go, but this conversation is not over. It won't be over until you come down off that high horse you're on and talk to me without all that animosity.'' She turned and headed for the door, her back stiff with anger.

Slade moved to the door ahead of her and pushed it open. ''Tell Rachel I'll be up in a few minutes.''

Shooting him a dark look, Tracy lifted the jacket over her head and began to move past him. Why was he so hard, so unbending? She wanted peace with Slade Dawson, or at least some sort of truce. For a fraction of a heartbeat, Tracy faltered. She froze in midstep and peeked up past the jacket. ''Slade—'' she breathed.

Her scent tantalized him, her nearness evoking a parade of unbidden challenges. Damn, she was beautiful...and special. And to realize just how special could be hurt. But it could never be. ''Don't,'' he mumbled, denying the light in her eyes.

Tracy stiffened, then scooted out into the rain. Had she heard revulsion in his voice? she wondered. She shivered uncontrollably, sure she'd heard something she wished she hadn't. Why would he despise her so much? And why did she keep picking up those electrically charged emotions from him?

Tracy darted to the house, running through puddles that were already deep enough to ruin her shoes. And she was nearly drenched when she reached the back door. Rachel was waiting. "Good God, girl, don't you know enough to stay out of the rain? Here, give me that...." Pulling the jacket away from Tracy, Rachel recognized it. "Slade's?"

Tracy nodded and shivered. "He's at the horse barn. He said to tell you he'll be up in a few minutes."

"Good, he's back. Now you, young woman, get up those stairs and into some dry clothes." Tracy was only too happy to comply and was halfway up the stairs when she heard Rachel yell, "Dinner will be on the table in a half hour, Tracy."

"Thank you!" she called back. In her room, her teeth chattering, Tracy pulled her wet clothes off and dug through a suitcase for a warm robe. The temperature must have dropped thirty degrees in as many minutes, she marveled, tying the sash of the pale blue velour robe tightly around herself. The same suitcase yielded a white cotton sweater and black-and-white houndstooth slacks, and she laid them on the bed, turning to very necessary cosmetic repairs before dressing.

While she tended to her makeup and hair, her mind was full of the events of the last few minutes. She had outwaited Slade, and there was a degree of satisfaction in that fact. But what had she really accomplished?

She'd learned a few odd facts. It was odd that Jase had never been to the ranch. But she still didn't know why he had retained fifty percent of a business he hadn't cared about enough to see.

There was more to it, Tracy concluded, a lot more. Slade was hiding something, and so were Rachel and Ben.

Did it have something to do with the ranch's management? Money, perhaps? Slade had been very defensive when he'd dared her to challenge his supervision. Oh, surely the "secret" didn't encompass anything underhanded in reporting profits, did it?

Frowning, Tracy stared at her mirrored reflection. She knew beyond a doubt that these people weren't thieves. Whatever they were guarding so determinedly wasn't anything criminal.

She had wasted nearly a week, so a few more days wouldn't matter. She would do exactly as she'd told Slade she would, stay until he talked to her in a normal, forthright manner. And if he didn't like it, that was his problem.

As for the chemistry she felt in his presence, that was her problem. They both had something to overcome.

Slade saw Rachel waiting for him when he came in the back door. Her voice was low and worried-sounding. "I'm glad you're back. Slade, what are you going to do about Tracy?"

He hung his wet hat on a hook behind the door and shook his head. "Nothing. She'll leave pretty soon."

"I don't think you should count on that. Slade, I think you should tell her the truth."

"No." The word had the ring of finality.

"You're misjudging her," Rachel protested softly. "She'd understand."

"Absolutely not."

"Why not? Be reasonable. She's curious, Slade, and with good reason." Slade groaned as Rachel eyed him with a developing suspicion. He had a right to protect his past, and if he told Tracy the whole story, she would despise him. Deep down Slade knew that he didn't want her hatred.

Rachel put her fingertips to her cheek. "Slade… you've got to put this thing to rest."

"I'm dealing with it. Don't worry about it." With a dark glower, Slade strode from the kitchen. There was something between him and Tracy. Maybe it was something neither of them had acknowledged yet, but it was there just the same.

Five

Tracy was stunned when she went down to dinner and discovered that Slade had "gone to town" again. Rachel seemed extremely embarrassed. She hurriedly apologized for Slade's bad manners, then said, "Ben won't be eating with us, either. He always has Saturday-night dinner with a lady friend. I told Slade he should stay and talk to you, honey, but he just wouldn't listen."

"It's all right, Rachel, I understand." She understood what he was doing, she just didn't understand why. Slade was going to avoid her whenever possible, and sitting down to dinner together might have looked like a concession on his part. His cold lack of consideration galled her, and she merely picked at Rachel's fine meal.

Maybe it was ridiculous, hanging around to talk to a man who made his aversion to conversation so plain. But how dare he treat her this way? Tracy couldn't remember ever being so deeply and abidingly angry with anyone. The memory of her attempt at friendship in the barn mocked her, underscoring Slade's disdain. "Maybe I should just go home," she said speculatively.

Rachel started, then said with a cautious gleam in her eyes, "I guess you've seen what you wanted to."

"The ranch? Oh, yes." There was a note of empathy in the housekeeper's voice, and Tracy gave her a probing look. "Rachel, it's obvious why Slade's not here tonight. He's doing everything he can to avoid me. Do you know why?"

Rachel put her fork down and sat back. Her round face expressed her discomfort. "Tracy, I wish you wouldn't ask me things like that."

"Why not? Can't you see how that sort of comment makes me feel?"

"Yes, I can. And I think you have a right to know everything. But it's just not my place to tell you."

"My God, what could be that bad?" Tracy tossed her napkin on the table. "Slade said Jase had never been to the ranch. Rachel, why would he keep a fifty-percent ownership in this place when he obviously didn't give two whits about it?" Her eyes narrowed. "You did meet Jase sometime in the past, didn't you?"

Rachel colored, and she stared at her plate in silence.

Tracy watched her across the table, then sighed. "All right, I'm sorry. I shouldn't press you when I know where your loyalties lie."

The muscles in Rachel's jaw worked. Slade was wrong. Tracy had every right to know the story, and for a moment Rachel was sorely tempted to blurt it out. Only a lifetime of loving Jemma and Slade Dawson prevented it, but the whole situation still didn't set right. She leaned forward, her eyes radiating the intensity of her feelings. "Ask Slade tonight, Tracy. When he comes in, make him tell you," she said ardently. "There's no reason he shouldn't—none that I can see—and I don't blame you for wondering. Wait up for him and pin him down. You have a right to know."

Rachel's dark eyes burned with an inner passion, and Tracy felt an odd fear. "It's something I really should know, isn't it?" she asked huskily.

"Yes, it is. Make him tell you," Rachel repeated soberly. "It will help you make a decision about the ranch, Tracy. You may not want to keep it."

The anger of the storm abated around ten that evening and settled into a peaceful rain. Tracy heard water pattering on the balcony roof and dripping from the eaves. She lay on the bed with the window cracked to get a little of the fresh, clean air into the room, and waited, with determination and a dozen scathing speeches in mind, for Slade to get home. Since Rachel's foreboding words, Tracy had undergone a transition, one that relegated Slade Dawson's "magnetism" to never-never land. Her feelings were put second in importance to learning what the Double J's secret was—and to the upcoming scene she anticipated.

She intended a full-scale showdown tonight, and it didn't matter whether it took place at midnight or four in the morning. She couldn't choose the hour. That was up to Slade. But she sure was going to choose the place. She listened intently for the sound of his truck, planning to run downstairs the moment she heard it.

Tomorrow morning she would call Brock McFee and arrange her pickup. By tomorrow night she would be back in San Francisco with all this behind her.

With a long sigh, Tracy turned over. She was still fully dressed and very uncomfortable. But slacks and a sweater were more sensible attire for this confrontation than a nightgown and a robe. Now that she had Slade in the proper perspective, she wanted to keep him there.

She checked her watch, which read 11:33, and fought the heaviness of her eyelids. Rachel was long asleep. Ben was out. The house was quiet. Rachel's encouragement came to mind again. She was on Tracy's side, if there actually were sides to take in the matter. Tracy couldn't fault the woman's refusal to speak. Her reticence was to be admired, since it was so obvious she disagreed with Slade's stubborn silence.

Tracy dozed, then awoke with a start. It was ten after twelve. She sat up and rubbed her eyes. Forcing herself off the bed, she went to the window and breathed the cold, tangy air.

What was Slade doing while she waited and stewed? A man with his looks certainly wouldn't lack for female companionship. Recalling Rachel's remark that "he got his share," Tracy frowned. No doubt he was spending his Saturday night with a woman. He probably wasn't worrying a bit that she was driving herself to the point of utter exhaustion trying to stay awake until he decided to come home.

Self-disgust hit her. He might stay out all night, and her watching a bleary-eyed sunrise wouldn't accomplish anything. Envisioning a four-in-the-morning confrontation was one thing, waiting for it was quite another. With an exasperated sigh, Tracy undressed, donned a peach-satin-and-ecru lace nightgown, turned back the blankets and crawled into bed. She dropped off to sleep almost instantly.

She awoke with a start, her pulse racing. Faint sounds from Slade's room betrayed his presence. She must have been subconsciously listening for his return. Tracy sat up and switched on the lamp to check her watch. It was 12:40. She'd slept only a half hour.

She jumped out of bed, regretting her weary decision to forgo confronting him tonight. This was her chance, and she was going to take it, no matter how he might try to get around it. As she drew on her warm robe, she could detect Slade's movements in the next room. She strained to hear, to decipher the footsteps and a vague rustling sound. What if he'd only come home for something and was already planning to leave again?

She wouldn't put it past him. He was so avid in his avoidance of her that she would have to take the opportunity even if it did mean going directly to his room. This discussion would have been better downstairs, no question about it, but she could deal with his bedroom.

Tracy stepped out onto the balcony. The chilly, damp air felt good and cleared her head of any remnants of drowsiness. A light shone from Slade's windows, and she peeked in. He was standing at a tall dresser, studying something, his back to her. Tracy stared, immediately wary. Slade was wearing jeans and nothing else.

Before she could react, caught for a moment between her determination to speak to him and a sudden, fearful suspicion that he might misinterpret her nocturnal visit, Tracy was startled to see him turn around and look directly at her. She almost ran, but Slade's expression of surprised disbelief stopped her.

She couldn't have him thinking she'd been merely window-peeking!

Gathering her wits, composing her features, she knocked on the glass and watched him walk across the room. Trying desperately to ignore his bare chest and the unbuckled belt at his waist, Tracy kept her eyes glued to his face, wincing inwardly at the steely gray of his eyes. His hair was tousled and rain-dampened. The wry smirk on his lips gave her pause. Obviously he didn't know what to make of this.

The French doors opened, and before Slade could speak, Tracy did. "I need to talk to you," she blurted.

"It's after midnight." Slade's frowning gaze slid down the blue robe and back up to her face. "Can't it wait till morning?"

"I'm leaving tomorrow," she said quickly. "And I have to talk to you."

Leaving? Slade's pulse leaped with both elation and an odd sense of loss. Still, he couldn't suppress a sardonic "You're leaving before dawn?"

Tracy flushed. "Of course not. But the way you continually disappear, I can hardly count on you being here."

He knew what this was all about. Tracy was set on finding out the truth before she left. Didn't the woman ever let up? She bothered him on another level, too, he admitted again, feeling her warmth and life much too intensely, knowing she'd been in bed, wondering what she had on under that robe. Her coming into his room wasn't a good idea. Didn't she know that? "I'll be here in the morning. We can talk then," he said gruffly.

"No! I don't have a lot of faith you'll be here, and I have to know some things." She was speaking louder than she'd intended, and she lowered her voice. "Rachel knows I planned to talk to you, so if she hears us, she won't be alarmed," she informed him. Then she blushed at the implication she heard behind her words.

Slade flushed, too, but more from being hemmed in than from anything else. Anger made him caustic.

"You shouldn't visit a man's room in the middle of the night."

Tracy's eyes widened. "I think we're adult enough to carry on a simple conversation, don't you?"

"Oh, we're adults, all right," he drawled with a cynical smile, wondering why she didn't see the danger. Maybe she didn't care. Something curled and leaped inside him, as it had the first time they'd been alone in the wee hours. He was only human. "All right," he growled, opening the door wider. "But I'm not promising anything."

Tracy stepped in. "I'm not asking for promises, just some honesty for a change."

"Honesty?" Slade walked over to the bed. He sat down, watching her through amused but wary eyes. "What's so urgent it can't wait till morning?"

Tracy was still standing. "I think you know."

"Your dear departed husband," he snorted.

"Yes."

Slade leaned back against the headboard and put his feet up on the bed. "I told you I never met the man. Do you think I lied about that?"

"I don't know what to think. That's why I'm here." Tracy looked around the room, finding Slade's bedroom intriguing. It was very masculine, almost stark. Her glance swept the plain, heavy dressers and the massive bed. She met his gaze. "I'd like to go home in the morning, but I'm not going without some answers. I think the ball's in your court. If you don't want me to stay longer, which you've made rather obvious, all you have to do is level with me."

He hadn't even offered her a chair. There was only one, and it contained his discarded shirt. His lack of manners was irritating. With a daggerlike glance in his direction, Tracy picked up the shirt, wondering where to put it. "Just toss it over here," he said, holding out a hand to catch it. With a look of rebuke, she brought the shirt to the bed and dropped it, wishing he'd put it on, and returned to the chair.

"What makes you so damned suspicious?" Slade muttered.

"*You* do," Tracy replied sharply as she sat down and made sure the robe was closed over her legs. "And Rachel, and even Ben. You know, if there's something going on here that you all prefer me not to know, why did you do things to make me curious?"

Slade's expression revealed nothing. "Like what?"

Tracy's eyes snapped. "Like your utter rudeness from the moment I arrived. Like Rachel's refusal to answer a simple question about Jase's visits to the ranch. Like—"

Slade interrupted her coldly. "Are you sure you're not just imagining things?"

"Are you suggesting I am? I told you before not to assume I'm stupid. You know damn well I'm not imagining things, and it's an insulting insinuation." Tracy spoke coldly, too.

They glared at each other. "Tell me the truth, Slade. Tell me about Jase's connection with the Double J. How was he involved here?"

Abruptly Slade swung his feet to the floor. "Maybe I don't want to," he muttered.

"And you have the nerve to tell me I'm imagining things? Good Lord, what's so terrible you can't talk about it?"

To Slade she didn't look like an interrogator. She looked kitten-soft and feminine in that robe. Her hair was lightly mussed, a cloud around her face, and her eyes were confused. A burning knot of resentment ignited in Slade's gut. "How come you married an old man?" he spit.

"What?" Startled, Tracy sat back, recoiling with shock. Slade didn't answer. He just kept staring. "Why would you ask me that?" she whispered hoarsely.

"Didn't you think I might wonder about it after the other night?" he countered cruelly.

"He wasn't old. How can you say such a thing? You didn't even know him." Tracy looked away from the piercing light in Slade's eyes. "And I didn't come in here to discuss...the other night. It should never have happened. I don't know why it did."

"You can't be as naive as you're letting on." Slade stood up and walked around the room. The lamplight glistened on the sleek tanned skin of his back and shoulders. He was deeply agitated, and his muscles were taut, his pacing erratic. "It could happen again. Right now! It could have happened this afternoon in the barn. Don't tell me you don't know that!"

Swallowing hard, Tracy watched him cautiously. "It has nothing to do with Jase," she whispered.

"Why in hell do you think I left that morning?" Slade raged quietly, as though she hadn't spoken. He turned to her. "Why did you think I left?" he asked tensely.

"I didn't know why," she confessed. "But I suspected it had something to do with what you and everyone else refuse to talk about."

Slade smirked. "It sure wasn't because I wasn't tempted by your beautiful body, lady," he said flatly, then shook his head. "It's probably not very smart of me to say this, but that scene on the balcony hasn't left my mind for a minute."

She froze, staring at him wide-eyed. Why was he confessing that now? This wasn't what she wanted to talk about. Was this a clever change of subject to throw her off the trail with the one topic she would find difficult to deal with?

Suddenly she felt the same turbulent electricity that had drawn them together that first night. Time stopped moving as they stared at each other. The rain seemed louder. It had a cocooning effect that formed a mesmerizing background for their escaping emotions. She saw him take a step toward her and then stop. Something in his eyes revealed an inner battle.

"Go back to your own room," he said in a tortured whisper. "Get the hell out of here before—"

Her legs wobbly, Tracy rose slowly. The scene had a slow-motion quality, and she felt strangely disoriented. It was only a few steps to the balcony, yet it seemed a mile. Her thoughts were muddled, encompassing the overpowering magnetism between them and how evasive Slade had been. She would leave without ever learning the truth, and she would wonder forever what had caused Slade's illogical behavior. Nearly to the door, she turned. "You're not going to tell me about Jase, are you?" she asked, her voice tremulous.

His fist clenched. The situation was so cruel that Slade could only handle it with anger. That he had fallen for this particular woman, that he *knew* he wanted her more than any other woman he'd ever known, caused a painful bitterness in his gut. Yes, he'd caused it himself. Fate had only played out the hand he had dealt when he'd foolishly plotted a small revenge on a cold, unfeeling man, a man he'd never met, a man he'd known only from an old photograph.

The picture! He'd been looking at it when he'd heard Tracy, and it was still lying on the dresser. Slade darted a glance to the large mahogany bureau and realized simultaneously that Tracy probably wouldn't know who the two people were if she did happen to see the photo. Jemma Dawson and Jason Moorland were eternally young in the snapshot. Two broad smiles, arms around each other. No, it wasn't likely Tracy would recognize her husband. Slade let his gaze return to her. Tracy looked forlorn, an unknowing participant in one of life's great farces, and his body ached to console her. He took another step forward. "It's nothing you need to know," he said gruffly. "You're leaving tomorrow. Go home and forget you were ever here."

"Forget what? A week of utter confusion? You're

a cold bastard, Slade, and you've been taking something out on me that I don't even know about.'' Tracy blinked to avoid the tears that threatened. "Maybe it's made you feel better, but it sure hasn't done me any good!'' Blindly she turned to go and stumbled toward the door, unable to keep the hot tears back any longer. She felt him behind her, and his hand on her arm brought her up short.

"Tracy—'' The word was an agonized whisper.

Through a blur of tears, she focused on the dark hair on his chest, her breath catching. "Please,'' she whispered, tugging against his grasp, not wanting him to see her cry.

"I—I'm sorry.'' Slade's lips moved against her ear. "I'm sorry,'' he whispered passionately. "You never should have been a part of this. You have nothing to do with it.''

Her head lifted sharply, the tears coursing down her cheeks forgotten. "A part of what? Tell me, for God's sake!'' His face looked tormented. And he was so close, touching her, one hard, sinewy thigh against hers, strong fingers gripping her arm. Suddenly it sunk in that he'd apologized, and with feeling. The anger in her shrank, became tolerable. "I don't know what to think about all this,'' she whispered.

He was silent a moment, his gaze searching hers. "Sell me your share of the ranch,'' he said softly.

"Sell it?'' Confusion racked Tracy, and she stood without moving. "Are you serious?''

"Yes. The accountants can decide what it's worth and I'll raise whatever it takes. Sell it to me, Tracy.

Let me have the Double J. It doesn't mean anything to you.''

A new deluge of questions hit her. "Did you try to buy it from Jase?"

Slade pulled back. "No."

"I'm very confused," she said weakly. "I can't give you an answer just like that. I'll have to think about it—at least a little."

"*Will* you think about it?"

She nodded. "Yes, I can promise that."

"Will you let me know when you decide?"

"Yes, I could do that, too." Amazed at the switch in topics and aware that Slade was guardedly watching her, Tracy drew a deep breath and reached for the doorknob. "Maybe if you owned it all you wouldn't be so secretive," she mused aloud.

"Maybe not," he agreed softly.

Tracy whirled. "That would be a condition, Slade. If I let you buy me out, I would want to know everything you do about Jason, every little detail."

His eyes narrowed. "Did you really love him?" he asked, his tone disparaging.

She hadn't expected such a question, not from Slade, and her bewilderment showed. "What a strange question," she said quietly. "Does that matter to you?"

Slade's expression was hard. "You're young, you're beautiful, you're intelligent. Maybe I can't quite believe you really loved an old man."

"He *wasn't* old! Yes, in years he was older than me, but Jase was full of life, active, energetic. Why

do you keep talking like he was ancient?'' Tracy's
eyes blazed as she spoke.

''Was he a good lover?''

''My God!'' she whispered, stunned by his crudity.
''Do you think I'm going to discuss that side of my
marriage with you?''

Slade's lips were curled cynically, and his eyes
were dark and hot. He moved quickly, without warning, and before she could react he'd pulled her up
against him, enclosing her with steely arms, pressing
his length to her. ''Was he?'' he whispered, forcing
her head back and looking directly into her eyes.
Something was driving him, and while he hated it, he
couldn't stop it. He wanted her to tell him she hadn't
loved Jason Moorland. He needed to hear it, and not
even the frightened look on her face could calm him.
''Was he?''

She was breathing hard, taking fearful breaths that
pushed her breasts into his bare chest. She felt a
churning in her loins, an echo of what he had caused
on the balcony. The pupils of his eyes were pinpoints
of diamondlike brilliance, boring into her, demanding
an answer. He inched their bodies closer together and
ground his hips forward, and she gasped at the sensation of his arousal pushing into her abdomen.

''Did you really love him?'' he whispered insis-
tently. His head came up, and his eyes closed tight,
an expression of pure pain on his face. ''Why did you
ever come here?'' he muttered.

Tracy knew he wanted her and knew he was battling it. Why? She stared up at him, more confused

than ever. She was held fast, barely able to move, as though he couldn't stop himself from holding her but was fighting a private war over it. "Slade, what's wrong?"

"Oh, God," he groaned, and brought his mouth to her hair. "I want you so much," he whispered hoarsely. "I had to leave before. I couldn't let this happen. I thought you'd go home. Why didn't you?"

"I told you why," she said softly, her mouth moving on his chest. The hair bristled against her cheek, and she moved her face enough to feel its coarse prickles, sending a wave of shivers up her spine. She wanted to stop his torment, and she snuggled closer, feeling a sharp, crazy joy at the knowledge that he wanted her. Whatever was creating his doubts had nothing to do with her. She was assailed by the same need and desire she'd felt before for this man. "I'm leaving tomorrow," she whispered, saying what was in her heart by melting into him.

"Tracy—" His voice was hoarse, guttural. "Maybe I'm too weak, but—" He pushed her head back and raised her chin to look at her "—I want to kiss you." He brought his mouth down on hers. The kiss dissolved all restraint, and they exploded into a frenzied passion.

She knew he was undressing her, but her eyes stayed closed. The robe fell away, and the straps of the nightgown slipped down her arms. His mouth left hers to adore her breasts, and his tongue lapped eagerly, his breathing loud and rasping. Then the gown was a small heap on the floor and he was sweeping her up into his arms. He was anxious, caught in a storm. When she was on his bed, he kicked his jeans off. Naked, splendid, achingly aroused, he straddled her hips. "Tracy, you're so beautiful, so beautiful," he whispered, running his hands over her breasts and down to the narrow expanse of her waist.

It had happened so fast. One moment they were arguing, the next she was in his bed. And it didn't matter.

Nothing mattered but the unbearable ache in her body. From the moment she had first seen Slade Dawson she had wanted him, Tracy realized dizzily, not even attempting to reconcile this unbelievable deviation from her usual standards. She had never met a man she couldn't resist before. She had no control where he was concerned. Reaching up to his neck, she pulled him down to her. "Kiss me. Make love to me," she whispered thickly.

He groaned and covered her lips, his mouth open, his tongue probing and hot. He moved between her willing thighs and slid into her, thrusting deep into her moist heat. Their kisses grew more feverish as control diminished and their movements became more frenetic. Gasping for air, he tore his mouth from hers and grasped her hips.

The room spun dizzily, and the crazy, wonderful rhythm rocking their bodies canceled even the most elemental thought. It was a rocket ride to the stars, wild, drugging. When it was over, when Slade weighted her down and they lay unmoving at last, reality was slow in returning.

At first, an utter peace gripped Tracy's mind. She felt surrounded, by weight, by male bulk, by sensual cloud. Then amazement set in. Never had she experienced such intense pleasure from a man. They had coupled like young animals, freely, without a trace of restraint. She had given everything, had wanted to give everything, but she had received, as well. Slade had also given everything.

As she marveled at the intensity of their lovemaking, tactile sensation returned and her fingertips began a slow exploration of his sweat-slicked back and shoulders. She felt his reaction, a renewed awareness, and Slade slowly lifted his head.

Their eyes met.

Neither spoke, neither smiled. Her fingers stopped moving on his back while they studied each other. Slade's tongue flicked, wetting his lips. What did he want her to say? They'd both known it would happen eventually. There were too many sparks between them for them not to have known right from the first.

This is still wrong, Slade thought. God, if she knew the truth...

A terrible pain invaded his body and reached his eyes. Tracy saw it, and the expression in her eyes grew questioning. "Slade?" she whispered, suddenly fearful.

She had to think this meant nothing, and he knew he had to convince her. Flippancy was the only answer. A forced smile curved his lips. "You're some sexy woman," he growled.

Tracy concealed the immediate and heartrending

hurt she felt. To Slade, this was a roll in the hay. And, yes, that was how she should see it too. Powerful chemistry didn't necessarily involve emotions. She could be as cool as he. Her smile was forced, but no one could have known. "If I am, you bring it out," she quipped lightly.

Slade watched her guardedly. Thank God she wasn't going to make a big deal out of this. Was she really leaving in the morning? He frowned. She wasn't satisfied with what she knew of Jason Moorland's involvement with the Double J, but perhaps her attention had been diverted enough that she wouldn't bring it up again. Besides, he could easily and excitedly keep her busy until morning. He'd already done the unthinkable. Would a long night of incredible lovemaking make his crime any worse?

He became gentle and smoothed the damp curls from her face. "You're a beautiful woman," he whispered, forgetting he just called her "sexy." She was sexy, but her beauty went beyond that. It touched him much too deeply. *She* touched him much too deeply.

She must never know.

Sighing, he brought his lips to her face and kissed a warm trail over her soft, satiny skin.

Surprised, sensing his intentions, Tracy debated with herself. She should…she shouldn't.

Her eyelashes fluttered downward, reflecting her decision. She would. She had to. Her fingers wound through the thick, dark hair at the back of Slade's neck while a sigh of acquiescence reached his ears.

He took her lips. Eagerly.

Six

How could a thinking woman merely feel? That was what Tracy knew she was doing. But her few isolated thoughts were so vague they were barely noticed.

Slade made her senses sing and her body respond like a beautiful musical instrument. The explosive passion of their first mating was gone but not forgotten, Tracy noted dreamily while Slade's hands moved over her. In its place was a consuming sensuality, an almost relaxed teasing that was every bit as rewarding. He was very gentle for someone who seemed to be emotionally uninvolved, she realized, sighing with sweet delight at the sensations he so easily maintained at a feverish pitch.

How could hard, callused hands touch so tenderly? They brushed her skin like the flutter of a butterfly's wing. But they had a man's knowledge. He was as loving as a lover—as a man in love—and that thought came through loud and clear, startling Tracy to keener awareness.

She watched the play of emotions on his face. She was seeing a side of Slade Dawson she wondered if even he knew he possessed. He put on such a hard front, such a tough, cynical face for the world. But she had instinct and intuition, and her inner voice told her few people saw the tenderness he was capable of.

He made love with the lights on. At first, swept along on a hot tide, neither of them had noticed or cared. Afterward, Tracy mentioned the lamps and Slade growled a hoarse "Leave them on. I want to see you."

And see her he did, with a studied concentration that would have made her blush if she hadn't been so involved in a similar examination. He was as she'd known he would be, taut, muscular, lean. Pure male, from his dark, unruly mop of hair to his long, narrow feet. His skin was tanned only from the waist up, evidence that he worked without a shirt; evidence too, that he didn't have time to worry about a perfect tan.

That was a far cry from the men she knew, Tracy acknowledged, running her hand down one long, sinewy thigh. She wondered if he'd ever even held a tennis racket and almost giggled at the improbability of him donning a pair of white tennis shorts.

What Slade had didn't come from aerobics or jogging or watching calories. His litheness came from hard physical labor, from long hours in the saddle, from making sure the Double J was an outstanding cattle ranch. Yes, he was different, but wasn't it that very difference that drew her?

"What are you thinking about?" Slade hadn't planned to ask such a dangerous question. Yet it had popped out, and it was too late to retract it. He was lying beside her, one thigh thrown across her, marveling at the symmetry of her body. There was a speculative look in her eyes.

They had spoken very little, and the question surprised and pleased Tracy. She smiled softly. She had no problem with the truth. "You."

"Trying to figure out what makes me tick?"

"Maybe. Do you mind?"

"Maybe." Yes, the question had been dangerous. It could lead to subjects better left alone. The whole idea of talking was dangerous, and to preclude it he bent his head and pressed his lips to hers.

God, she was sweet. Her mouth was warm and soft and tasted like wine. At least it was as drugging as good wine. He drank of it thirstily, probing the heady moisture behind her lips with a searching tongue. He wanted her again, and it was mind-boggling to realize she didn't object. She was pliant, curious, an incredibly loving woman.

Was she this way with other men?

The dark thought was disturbing, and he tore his mouth from hers and brought his head down to her breasts. He could hear her heartbeat. It was a quick flutter, matching the soft little breaths she was taking.

Why was she doing this? The first time was understandable—they had both been caught in a sensual storm. But now? She made no move to leave his bed, and Lord help him, he was glad.

Anger at the unholy implications of what he was doing created an ache in Slade's mind. He couldn't blame Tracy for this. For being on the ranch, yes. For intruding on his life, for being a Moorland, yes. But not for this. This was all his doing, but, God have mercy, he couldn't help himself.

Could any man?

The emotional excuse offered little real consolation, and Slade forced it from his mind. He would have tonight and worry about tomorrow, tomorrow.

He cupped a breast, closed his mouth around it, feeling at once her swift intake of air. He affected her strongly, but no more than she affected him. There was an incredible chemistry between them, something he had never experienced with another woman, even though there had been other women in his life. Yet he had never been in love.

Why hadn't he ever felt this warm, sinking sensation for a woman he could have? Why feel it now, for a woman he could never have?

Forget it, he told himself angrily. Take what you can. Forget everything else. He slid a hand between her thighs, and Tracy's gasp of pleasure made his blood surge. They might never have anything else together, but they would both remember tonight.

This time, when he claimed her body, he rested on his forearms and watched her reactions. The glow in her deep green eyes became irresistible, and he moved his hips slowly, sustaining the pleasure for as long as possible.

In the end, it was as wild as the first time, and he knew the scratches on his back would be visible for days to come. Beneath him, Tracy lay without moving, her eyes closed, breathing softly, serenity on her face. She startled him by whispering, "I've been to the other side of the moon."

He lifted his head to see her, wanting to confess the same. What the hell, why not? It was true. "It was the best."

She sighed, opened her eyes and smiled. Soft fingertips caressed his face. "You're a very special man, Slade." Her voice was husky, daring an emotional confidence.

He swallowed hard. At a moment when they should be basking in love's afterglow, whispering the truth about their lovemaking, he had to be on guard. He had to kill any developing feelings for him she might be entertaining. It was easier to do when he remembered how she would despise him if she knew everything. "Not so special," he said, the expression in his eyes unreadable. He took in a sharp breath, then said, "This has to stop here, Tracy."

"Does it?" Tracy's eyes widened. Surely he wasn't serious, she thought. Why did it have to stop here? They were consenting adults and certainly weren't hurting anyone else. True, sleeping with a man she didn't know very well maybe wasn't the smartest thing she'd ever done. And yes, there was still that damnable "secret" between them. But after the wonder of their lovemaking, how could he say such a thing? "Can it?" she whispered hoarsely.

A shudder shook his body. "It has to."

Confusion racked her. The wall he'd briefly let down was back in place, blocking her out again. For a painful moment she felt used, but she quickly denied the feeling. What they'd shared couldn't be categorized so coldly. Slade hadn't used her, any more than she had used him. What had taken place on this bed had been more than just a need for physical release; it had been a mutual explosion. There had been real feeling between them, and he could deny it till doomsday and not convince her.

Still, his declaration left her feeling vulnerable.

"Will I ever understand you?"

"It doesn't matter if you do or not," he mumbled. Sensing the pain he'd just inflicted and recoiling from it, Slade rolled away from her and got off the bed. Stunned, Tracy watched him reach for his jeans.

The phone rang shrilly, intruding on the tension-filled moment. With a frown and a glance at the digital clock on the nightstand, Slade grabbed the phone. "Hello!" he barked, angry with whoever had the nerve to call at three in the morning, angrier still with the interrupted situation and taking it out on the caller.

Then he paled and Tracy sat up.

"When? Where? I'll tell her," he said quietly. "Thank you." He put the phone down. "That was the hospital. Ben's been in an accident. I've got to tell Rachel." Zipping his jeans as he went, he ran from the room.

While she scrambled into her nightgown and robe, Tracy could hear Slade's and Rachel's voices down the hall. In minutes Slade was back and he rushed to finish dressing. "Is it bad?" Ben and Rachel had become very important to her, Tracy realized with almost paralyzing fear.

"I don't know. He's in the emergency room. We're going to Helena right away."

She watched him pull his boots on, icy fingers clutching her heart. "May I come along?"

Slade looked surprised. "Do you want to?"

"That's better than staying here and worrying. Do you think Rachel would mind?"

"No, she wouldn't. Hurry, though. I want to leave right away."

Tracy nodded and dashed through the door Slade had left open. She collided with Rachel in the hall. "Oh, Tracy! Did Slade tell you?"

Fighting an embarrassed flush, Tracy nodded. "Yes. I'm coming with you, Rachel. I'll just be a minute." Cursing her carelessness in rushing into the hall instead of using the balcony, Tracy hurried to get ready. She hastily dressed in the slacks and sweater she'd worn earlier and went downstairs to where Slade and Rachel were waiting.

They left the house and climbed into Slade's pickup. Tracy sat in the middle, and Slade drove. The rain had stopped, but the highway was covered with a thin layer of water that diffused the headlight's illumination and made it difficult to see. Tension filled the cab.

Slade and Rachel talked around her as if she weren't there. "Don't think the worst," Slade warned. "He may be just fine."

"I wish they'd have told you more," Rachel said anxiously.

"They didn't know more. They will by the time we get there."

"Yes, of course. But I wonder if he was alone." Despite Slade's admonition not to worry in advance, Rachel was understandably upset. "I wonder if Carol was with him."

Tracy assumed "Carol" was Ben's lady friend and kept silent, resting her head on the back of the seat. She was worried, too, but Rachel didn't need to hear that. She was also very tired, she realized. So she let Rachel and Slade's conversation drift around her, and she absorbed little of it. Aware of Slade beside her, furtively enjoying the sensation of his heavy, hard thigh touching hers, of his arm brushing hers as he drove, it was easy for her to let her thoughts return to his bedroom.

Slade didn't feel like a stranger any longer, but that was to be expected. More to the point, she felt as if a ton of bricks had been dropped on her in the last week, knocking her for an emotional loop. The oddest feeling of all to assimilate was the sense that this was real. Riding in a pickup truck through the Montana darkness with Slade Dawson at the wheel, feeling the heat of his body reaching out to her, didn't seem the least bit out of place.

Could she leave Slade now to return to the city?

He'd said it had to end here, but it seemed such a groundless statement and a direct contrast to the feelings he conveyed. Why was he torn? What had Jase done here to make Slade so wary?

Instantly Tracy realized she was blaming Jase for whatever was wrong, and she stirred uneasily. She felt Slade glance at her and gave him a small smile. He looked away immediately, but in the light from the dash she caught a flash of concern. Was it for Ben or for them?

Lord, what she'd like to do right this minute was put her arms around him and tell him not to worry, that everything would be all right. But with Rachel in the truck she didn't dare. Even though when Rachel was eventually able to think of something other than Ben she'd no doubt remember her coming out of Slade's room at three in the morning.

Tracy sighed and closed her eyes. It might be best for Rachel to realize she and Slade were on different terms. Maybe then Slade could stop being so darned secretive.

Slade's offer to buy her out came to mind. She would give it some serious consideration, discuss it with her accountants, although the idea of giving up every tie to Montana was less appealing than it might have been a few days before. She didn't want to think about cutting herself off from Slade.

She nodded drowsily, and the next thing she knew the truck was stopping. Sitting up straighter, Tracy realized she'd fallen asleep and had naturally made herself more comfortable against Slade's shoulder. He appeared not to have noticed and jumped from the truck while Tracy slid out Rachel's side. They hurried into the hospital.

The bright lights of the emergency room were blinding, and Tracy blinked at the sudden glare. Slade went to the desk. "We had a call about Ben Munley," he told the woman on duty.

"Yes, Mr. Munley is here. One moment, please, and I'll check on his status." The woman disappeared, and Slade turned to Rachel.

"Easy," he said softly, seeing the near-panic on her face.

The woman returned. "Are you all family?"

"I'm his sister," Rachel volunteered shakily.

"You may see him, then."

Rachel looked at Slade, fear in her eyes. Slade took her arm. "I'm going, too," he announced firmly.

"I'll wait out here," Tracy offered, and the woman nodded.

"All right. Through that door, room 3."

The waiting room was deserted, and Tracy chose a couch, preparing herself for a long wait. But when the receptionist looked up and smiled, she stood up again and walked to the desk. "I'm not family, but I'm very concerned about Mr. Munley. Is he all right?"

"He was in a car accident, miss."

"Yes, I know that."

"All I can tell you is that they've taken X rays and several doctors have seen him."

Tracy smiled weakly. "Thank you." She returned

to the couch, slipped her shoes off and put her feet up. Poor Ben. Poor Rachel! They were very close and Tracy knew that if Ben was seriously injured it would devastate his sister.

She fell asleep worrying about Ben—and Slade.

"Wake up, Tracy."

She opened her eyes and looked up to see Slade. She sat up and slid her feet into her shoes. "Is Ben all right? Where's Rachel?" It was still very early, but the sun was up.

"She's upstairs. Ben's in the operating room."

Tracy's heart sank. "What for, Slade?"

"A ruptured spleen. He's got several broken ribs and a broken leg. He's badly bruised and has a concussion too. I'm going for coffee. Would you like some?"

"Yes, thank you. He's going to be okay, isn't he?" Tracy stood.

"The doctors think so. He'll be in some danger for a few days, but they're optimistic."

"Thank God!" They walked down a long corridor, following the signs to the cafeteria. "Is Rachel all right?"

"I think so. She didn't want to leave the OR waiting room, and I told her I'd bring her some coffee." He took her arm and steered Tracy to the coffee urn. With two large cups of hot coffee, they went to a table and sat down.

Slade looked gray, and Tracy watched him as she sipped. "You're exhausted, aren't you?"

"It's been quite a night," he replied quietly, giving her a long look.

She flushed but nodded her understanding. "I'm so sorry about Ben," she said. "He'll be in the hospital for a long time, won't he?"

"Probably."

"Do you know what happened?"

Slade nodded. "One of the doctors told me. It was raining hard and a truck passed him. I guess the water must have blinded him, because he braked too suddenly and the pickup went into a skid and flipped."

Tracy shuddered. "He could have been killed."

"Yes, very easily."

For a few moments they were both silent. Slade spoke first. "Are you still leaving today?"

She smiled. "I guess it is today, isn't it?" The smile faded, and she met Slade's gaze. "Do you want me to go?"

He looked away. "Don't do that," he said tersely.

"I have to do that. Do you want me to leave today, Slade?" He didn't answer, just sat tight-lipped, staring off across the nearly empty cafeteria. "Can't you tell me?" she asked softly. "If you leave it up to me, I'll stay. You know that, don't you?"

"For God's sake, Tracy!"

"You simply cannot be honest with me, can you? Why not, Slade?" Her voice was low, pain-filled.

"You don't know what you're asking," he said bitterly.

She shook her head. "No, I know I don't. All I really know is what happened tonight. And I know you weren't unaffected, Slade, no matter how much you want me to believe that.'' Tracy held her cup with both hands, noticing the tremble in her grasp. ''Am I wrong?''

His head jerked around and he stared across the table, his eyes dark and turbulent. ''Yes, you're wrong!'' Abruptly he got up. ''Come on, let's go.''

She drew a troubled breath. ''You go ahead. I'll be up in a few minutes.'' Slade whirled and walked away, and she watched him get another cup of coffee, place a cover on it and leave the cafeteria. He absolutely was not going to acknowledge the possibility of real feelings, no matter what she did.

What had happened to make him so bitter? Weakly Tracy sat back, realizing the situation's futility. Slade would make love to her, but he wouldn't let himself feel anything for her. It was both frustrating and hopelessly baffling. She sat and finished her coffee, taking her time but getting nowhere near a solution. When she got up and left the cafeteria, she was still trying to decide whether to go home as she'd planned. If she'd brought her things to Helena, Slade could have dropped her off at the airport. As it was, she'd have to return to the ranch and call for the helicopter.

She found Rachel and Slade on the second floor and gave Rachel a hug. ''Are you all right?'' she asked.

''I'm fine, honey. I was just telling Slade that I'm going to stay in Helena a few days. I want to be near Ben until he's out of danger.''

Tracy took a seat. ''Of course. I don't blame you.''

She glanced at Slade and saw only a taut, closed expression; felt his silent withdrawal. He had shut her out again, and it hurt like hell. Swallowing hard, she turned to Rachel again. "Is there anything I can do for you, Rachel, anything at all? Maybe something at the ranch? Errands, phone calls?"

Rachel thought a moment. "Well, you could gather up a few things for Slade to bring back to me." She smiled. "I think you'd know more what I need than he would."

"Gladly. Anything else?"

"Oh, gosh, honey, I can't think of anything right now. Are you going to be around a little longer? I thought you were leaving today."

"I was." Tracy gave Slade a defiant look. "But if you don't mind, Rachel, I'd like to stay a few more days, just until Ben's out of danger."

"Mind? Well, of course I don't mind. That's very thoughtful of you."

They all looked up as a man wearing OR green came in. "Miss Munley?"

"Yes," Rachel said, getting to her feet nervously. "Is Ben all right?"

"I'm Dr. Shively. Ben is in recovery now. You can see him in about an hour. We had to remove the spleen and do some repair surgery. He'll be in Intensive Care for at least one day because of the concussion, perhaps more. But things look good."

Rachel relaxed visibly and released a long-held breath. "Thank God." Slade had risen, and he put his arm around her shoulders.

"Only Rachel can see him?" he asked Dr. Shively.

"For today it would be best, yes."

Slade nodded. "All right."

"Wait about an hour, Miss Munley, then go to ICU. They'll let you see your brother." Dr. Shively smiled and left.

Rachel sat down again, obviously relieved. "He's going to be all right."

"Oh, Rachel, I'm so glad," Tracy said softly, and reached for Rachel's hand.

"They'll monitor him because of the concussion," Slade put in. "But after that he'll be moved to a regular room. Rachel, I think I'll go back to the ranch and check on the men. I'll come back tonight and bring your things."

"That's sensible," Rachel agreed. "There's no reason for you to stay when you can't see Ben. Tracy, you might as well go back, too. Pack me a small suitcase. Enough for a couple of days."

"All right." Tracy rose. "I'll get everything you need together."

"Thanks." Rachel stood slowly. "I'll walk down with you and get a breath of air. I've got an hour to kill before I can see Ben, and a little walk would feel good."

As they made their way to the first floor, Slade told Rachel he'd line up a motel room nearby for her before he left town. When they reached the pickup, Rachel stood with Tracy for a moment and spoke quietly. "Did you talk to Slade?"

The question took Tracy by surprise, and she stammered, "I—I tried, Rachel."

"This will give you the chance. He can't avoid you when you're driving down the road together." She grinned a little and stepped back from the truck. "Bye. See you later."

Slade's face was grim as they drove away from the hospital. Tracy sat as far away from him as the seat permitted, staring out the window. The hour-and-a-half ride back didn't promise to be very pleasant. Within a block, Slade turned into the parking lot of a motel, parked the truck and got out without a word.

Tracy sighed and shook her head. In a few minutes, Slade came out of the motel office and climbed back in also without speaking. He was being ridiculous, Tracy thought, irritated. "Did you get Rachel a room?"

"Yes," was his terse reply. The pickup started and they left the parking lot. It was still early, and traffic was light. They quickly left the city and reached the highway.

"Are you going to drive a hundred miles without talking?" Tracy asked, her voiced edged with anger.

"You want to talk?" Slade shot her a hard look. "All right, let's start with when you're planning to leave."

"You don't want to talk, you want to fight," she said accusingly.

"What I want is for you to get on a plane and get the hell out of Montana," Slade answered harshly.

"That's not what you wanted last night!"

"I don't turn it down when it's pushed in my face," he said coldly.

Tracy gasped. "Why, you conceited bastard! I didn't do that, and you know I didn't!"

Slade was staring straight ahead, his lips tight with tension. Anger was his only defense. Besides, he was so tired he was beyond putting up any kind of front. This thing with Tracy was impossible, so ironic it was almost laughable. Almost. "Tracy, just go home," he muttered wearily.

She stared daggers at him. "I wonder if you have any idea how I feel. I came here with the best of intentions and was verbally mistreated by you from the moment I arrived. If that wasn't enough to make me wonder what was going on, Rachel and Ben both intimated at some dark secret involving Jase. On top of all that, you do an about-face on the balcony and—"

"I didn't do it alone," he inserted sarcastically.

"No, you didn't. I accept full responsibility for my actions, but not for yours, Slade. What motivates you is the biggest mystery of the century. I've never met anyone who could run so hot and cold before."

He gave her a quick sidelong glance. "Changing your mind about me being special?" he drawled wryly.

"That's what you want, isn't it? For some crazy reason that's exactly what you want. I only wish you were man enough to tell me what the reason is."

"Think what you want."

"Oh, I will. I don't have any choice, do I?" Fum-

ing, Tracy faced front again, her arms folded across
her breasts belligerently. Right that moment she
wasn't feeling much kindness for Slade Dawson; the
emotion gripping her was much closer to hatred. And
frustration, and enough anger to want to return some
of the hurt he'd dished out. "There are other ways of
finding out what this is all about," she declared.

"Oh? What ways?"

"I could start with the accountants. I could hire a
detective to look into Jase's past. That might at least
tell me how he came to own part of the ranch." Tracy
felt triumphant when she saw Slade's discomfort. "It
would, wouldn't it?" she added, her eyes narrowed
thoughtfully.

"You might find out something you'd rather not
know."

Tracy scoffed. "I doubt that. I can't imagine Jase
doing anything so terrible I'd be shocked by it."

"He was so great, wasn't he?" Slade's mouth
twisted bitterly. "If he was, if all your memories are
so wonderful, how come you melt when I touch
you?"

"You hate him, don't you?"

"Yeah, I hate him. Jason Moorland was the biggest
son of a bitch that ever came down the pike."

She was momentarily speechless. Slade took his
eyes from the road and stared at her, his expression
menacing, looking away only when it was necessary.
"I don't suppose there's a ghost of a chance of you
telling me why you hate a man you never even met,"
she finally got out.

"Right this minute, I'm tempted," Slade threatened in a low, tense voice.

"Then do it! I'm half-crazy with all this innuendo and no facts."

"Tracy, I'm beat. Just shut up and leave me alone!"

Something in his voice rang a warning bell. Tracy looked out the side window, still silently fuming. Maddening as it was, she really didn't know Slade, and she certainly didn't know how far he could be pushed. From the angry set of his posture, she suspected he'd about reached the end of his patience.

Well, so had she. She'd had enough of Slade Dawson. The fact that they were physically wild for each other meant nothing. Her innate naiveté and her disinclination to believe she was capable of wanting sex with a man without love were making her construe lust as something meaningful. That was really all it had been, she decided. Pure lust. It was time to face that tasteless fact and accept it.

She did have one ace in the hole, though, and after an hour of stony silence she couldn't help playing it. "I've decided I'm not selling you my half of the ranch," she said smugly.

He only shot her another cold look.

"Did you hear me?"

"I heard. If that's your revenge, enjoy it."

"I intend to. What's more, I plan to visit my ranch several times a year."

Slade smirked bitterly. "Just let me know when you're coming so I can be gone."

A rush of tears choked her. "I hate you," she whispered, and turned away, totally defeated. Tracy wiped at the tears that kept dripping down her cheeks, furious at herself for being so weak as to let him see how clearly he'd beaten her.

Slade wanted to stop the pickup, and he even swerved toward the side of the road briefly. He wanted to put his arms around her and apologize and hold her. He wanted it so badly he ached. But the enormity of the entire affair, his past, who she was, who *he* was, stopped him. Let her think the worst, he decided. In the long run she'd be better off. If she ever did find out the truth, she'd thank him for halting this thing right here and now.

Even with tears on her face and no makeup, even with her hair less than perfect, Tracy was beautiful. He'd never find another woman like her, never. Jason Moorland's wife. It still didn't seem real to Slade. It was like a bad dream. Yet she wasn't a dream, she was warm flesh and very hot blood. What they'd shared wasn't a dream, either. She still looked soft and womanly, even though she sat so stiffly. The tiniest recollection of how she looked without clothes had the power to arouse him. Abruptly Slade rolled down his window and took a big breath of fresh air. They were almost to the ranch. Once they were there he'd be able to get out of this damn cab, get away from her.

He knew she was hurting. But she'd hurt a hell of a lot worse if she knew why he'd tried to avoid her. He never should have taken her to bed. Yet he wondered that he even had the strength to vow he wouldn't do it again when what he really wanted to do was stop the truck and lay her down right here.

He saw the ranch road with tremendous relief and turned onto it. The moment the pickup had stopped beside the house, Tracy jumped out and ran to the door. Slade got out slowly and started for the barns.

From the kitchen window, Tracy watched him go. She was so full of pain that she had to let the tears flow free. Emotions battled within her. Even now her pulse quickened at the sight of his long-legged stride, of his straight back tapering to narrow-hipped masculinity. "You bastard," she whispered, getting small satisfaction out of verbalizing her torment.

Seven

After a bath, Tracy packed a suitcase for Rachel, set it by the kitchen door and went up to bed. As agitated as she was, exhaustion won, and she fell sound asleep without ever hearing Slade come in.

He also bathed and fell into bed, dropping into a deep sleep immediately. He didn't hear Tracy get up at one that afternoon.

The big old house was quiet, and when she first awoke she thought Slade had already left for Helena. Still groggy, Tracy slipped into a robe and went downstairs. The suitcase was undisturbed, and Slade's pickup was parked outside. He was still on the ranch. Was he out with the men or upstairs in his room?

Her heart jumped erratically. Think! she commanded herself. Remember how cold and hateful he was!

It didn't work. She kept seeing him in bed: the lithe ranginess of his body, the intensity behind his eyes.

She sucked in a sharp breath. She had to go home. It was the only sane thing to do. She couldn't go on like this, hating him, desiring him. He was rude, crude and possibly a liar. He kept saying he'd never met Jase, but people didn't hate complete strangers.

Quickly, as though action could lessen the pain of her thoughts, she made a pot of coffee and went upstairs to dress while it was brewing. When she passed Slade's solidly closed door she noticed that all was quiet within. He must still be sleeping, which was easy to understand. He'd been up all night, doing Lord only knew what before he'd come home. Then they'd spent two hours together before they'd received Rachel's phone call. As he'd said in the cafeteria, it had been quite a night.

Knowing she should either catch a ride back to Helena with Slade or—more sensibly—call McFee's Charter Service, Tracy stood at the French doors in her room and stared out. It was oddly upsetting to face going home, but it was what she had to do.

And then what? Roiling emotions made her edgy, unsettled, and she pulled the door open. Yesterday's storm was over, leaving serene beauty in its wake. The air was so clean that it seemed to sparkle, and the trees, lawn and flowers looked freshly bathed, renewed. Tracy stepped out on the balcony and sighed longingly. If only *she* could be refreshed so easily. If only something could wash away the cloud of despair weighing her down as easily as the rain had cleansed the Double J.

She thought of the sleeping man, so near, yet so far, and pondered their relationship. She remembered the Jase she'd known and loved and tried to reconcile him with the man Slade had cursed. Nothing added up.

Small wonder she was in such a quandary, she acknowledged unhappily.

So she had no alternative but to leave the Double J and forget Slade Dawson. At that thought, Tracy's eyes grew misty. How could sane, sensible, citified Tracy Moorland ever have become enamored of a rough, crude Montana male? It didn't fit, any more than Jase's alliance here had. Yet each of them—she in a way she'd never have thought possible, and Jase because of his involvement in what was now a dark mystery—had found something on the Double J.

If only Slade were able to face her honestly. Jase's connection with the ranch, and Slade's low opinion of him, hadn't stopped Slade from making love to her. What was more, Tracy suspected, if she went to his room he'd make love to her again. She knew all she'd have to do was slip into bed with him and—

What would happen if she did that, if she quietly entered his room and lay beside him? Would he push her away?

Tracy's mouth went as dry as cotton. How could she contemplate such a thing? Did she enjoy punishment? No one could have been crueler or plainer than

Slade had been today. He wanted her to leave, to get out of his life. Yes, he might accept her in his bed again, but he'd probably do the same with any reasonably attractive woman.

Was that really true? she wondered. Was he as warm and tender with just any woman? She'd felt such an emotional communion in his arms. It couldn't have been merely imaginary.

Her chin came up. She'd never know any more than she knew right this minute—not about Jase, not about Slade. In a way, they were two peas from the same pod, both secretive, private men. Of course, she hadn't really realized the extent of Jase's privateness, not until his death.

There was no point in pressing Slade again. He wasn't going to talk and that was all there was to it. Tracy eyed her suitcases. Rachel would understand if she changed her mind about staying. In fact, she could call Rachel from San Francisco and speak to her about it in person.

She would call McFee. The thought of riding back to Helena with Slade's coldness was too much. Purposefully Tracy left her room to go downstairs to make the call. Using the kitchen phone, she dialed the number, waited through three rings and finally heard Brock McFee's cheery voice on the line.

Ten minutes later, she put the phone back in its cradle. It was done. Brock McFee would pick her up in two hours, and she also had a reservation on a flight from Helena to San Francisco. She rose slowly, despising the urge to shed tears, and poured herself a cup of coffee before she went back up the stairs to her room.

She chose traveling clothes, pearl-gray pleated slacks, a green-and-gray blouse and gray pumps and bag, adding a matching green jacket to the array on the bed just in case San Francisco was cool when she deplaned. Then, sipping coffee at intervals, she did her makeup and hair.

She stopped cold, the hairbrush frozen in midair, when she heard Slade's bedroom door open and then heard his footsteps in the hall. The door closed and it was quiet again.

Outwardly calm, she finished dressing. While buttoning her blouse, she heard Slade return to his room and a short time later go downstairs.

So be it. He would leave for Helena, and she would leave for San Francisco without even a goodbye. It was best. She was wearier of pleading and begging for information than he probably was of refusing to answer.

Tracy took her time. She gathered up the few possessions she had placed around the room, locked her suitcases and moved them to the hall. After a last look to make sure she'd forgotten nothing, she picked up the empty coffee cup and went downstairs.

Entering the kitchen, she stopped dead. Slade wasn't gone, he was sitting at the table with his own cup of coffee in front of him. He was freshly shaved and wearing a royal-blue shirt, and even his usually tousled hair was neatly in place. She recoiled from his disruptive image while his eyes raked over her.

Concealing her surprise, Tracy walked over to the coffeepot. "I thought you had already left," she said tonelessly, vowing to keep this unexpected meeting impersonal.

"There's no hurry," Slade replied in an equally unrevealing voice.

"No, I suppose not," she agreed, getting her coffee. She had intended using the phone. No matter, she could use the one in the study. Starting for the door, she turned. "Would you tell Rachel goodbye for me, please?"

"You're leaving?" The question was blunt, conveying nothing of the jolt her words had given him.

"Yes. Tell Rachel I'll call her from San Francisco." Tracy resumed her exit, ignoring her own nervousness. She made her way to the study, sat at the desk and put her mug down with an unsteady hand.

She wouldn't dwell on this, wouldn't allow it to shake her. Picking up the phone, she dialed a long-distance number. She was sure her father would be home. He usually was on Sunday afternoon. "Dad? I'm glad I caught you. I'll be arriving in San Francisco at 8:20 this evening. Could you meet me?"

Jim Kirkland was happy to comply. "I'm glad you're coming home, Tracy."

"Yes, me too."

She tried to sound interested in her father's conversation and even managed a few sensible comments. But her heart wasn't in it, and she was relieved to finally be able to say, "See you tonight, Dad," and put the phone down.

Then, listlessly, she stared into space, seeing nothing of the charming old room, the bookshelves, the rock fireplace. The Double J and the people she'd met here were hard to leave. She had entered a whole new world here, and it would forever be with her, no matter how many miles she put between it and herself.

"Tracy?"

She jumped and turned her gaze to the doorway. Slade was leaning against the frame, and she wondered how long he'd been watching her. "Yes?"

"Do you want a ride into Helena?"

She stood up. "No, thanks. I called McFee."

He nodded. "All right. I thought you probably had."

They had nothing to say to each other. They had never before shared a normal conversation, and they couldn't now. Small talk was impossible. But there was no denying their emotional communication. It made the air heavy, almost turbulent.

Tracy rounded the desk and took tentative steps toward the door. Slade never budged, but his eyes never left her. She looked beautiful, again expensively dressed, her hair and makeup perfect, just as she had when she'd stepped down from McFee's helicopter. Only she'd been wearing blue that day; now she was dressed in gray and a shade of green that echoed the unique color of her eyes. He found it impossible to breathe normally. "I...maybe..."

Her advance stalled. "Maybe what, Slade?"

There were things he'd wanted to say, but it had been a stupid impulse. He cleared his throat. "Nothing. I'll carry your luggage down.'' Turning, he disappeared from the doorway.

Tracy followed, staying several steps behind him as they descended the stairs. What had that been all about? The question beat in her brain, causing turmoil, stealing her composure.

She finally caught up with him. ''Just put it on the front porch for now,'' she suggested in a strained voice.

She looked at him, and her breath stopped at the cloud of pain she saw in his eyes. ''Don't look at me like that,'' she whispered.

''Like what?''

''Like—'' She broke off and looked away. She felt his hand on her arm and winced at the response she suffered at his touch.

''How was I looking at you?'' Slade's voice was ragged. He shouldn't be touching her. She was leaving. It was what he'd wanted all along, and he should be relieved. But the warmth he felt beneath the silk of her blouse, her magical scent, the tremor in her body that he knew was caused by him, it was all too heady to deny. He slid his hand up her arm to her shoulder, then through the mass of her hair to the back of her neck. ''What did you see?'' he whispered huskily.

She closed her eyes and moved her head, creating a shivering delight at the tingling abrasiveness of his hand on her neck. ''Why are you doing this? I know you're glad I'm going.''

''Maybe I'm not so glad.''

Her eyes flew open, and when she spoke her voice was tormented. "Slade—"

"Whatever I've done wasn't because of you," he said hoarsely. "Can you believe that?"

"Are you apologizing?" Their gazes were locked, a confusion of stormy emotions in each.

"Is that what you want? An apology? All right, you've got it. I'm sorry, Tracy, I won't ever forget you." His hand moved beneath her hair, kneading sensitive skin. "Not if I live to be a hundred."

Her expression softened. She wanted to be as hard as he'd been but couldn't. "I won't forget you, either." She reached up to touch his cheek gently. "I don't understand you," she confessed sadly.

"I know you don't. It's best that way." He studied her face for a moment, then slowly urged her closer with a tug on the back of her neck. "Let me kiss you goodbye," he whispered.

Startled, Tracy tried to pull away. "No!"

He put his arms around her. "I have to," Slade mumbled thickly. "Put your arms around me. Kiss me."

Tears filled her eyes. "Slade, don't do this. You're tearing me apart."

"Oh, sweetheart, if you only knew—" He took her lips hungrily. It wasn't a goodbye kiss, it was a kiss of passion, of longing. Tracy lifted her arms to his neck. Their bodies molded together, her soft breasts straining against his steely chest. His arousal was immediate, searing her even through layers of clothing.

They weren't saying goodbye, they were saying, "I

want you,'' and in the most elemental way. They were saying, ''I have to have you'' with hot kisses and searching tongues, and with Slade's hands holding her hips to his.

She felt despair, and wonder. She had no control with him. How could she be so wild for a man unless she loved him? Love... Did she *love* this heartless man? Could she?

A whimper rose in her throat, yet she couldn't tear her mouth from his. His kiss was wet, openmouthed, demanding, his tongue an erotic invader. She clung to his thrilling bulk, giving him everything he asked and more.

Panting, they stared into each other's eyes. Slade's were glazed with desire. It was evident from the hot light in his eyes that he wanted much more than a kiss.

But so did she. Did it matter that she was dressed and ready for flight? Did it matter that her makeup was already ruined and her hair disheveled? When he swung her up into his arms as though she weighed nothing and took long, hurried strides into his bedroom, nothing mattered.

They undressed with a shared urgency, tending to their own buttons. He was naked first, splendid, so beautiful her hands stopped. He stepped closer. ''Let me,'' he said, and slid her cream colored satin underpants down.

Then they were in his bed and his mouth was traveling her body. She closed her eyes to the delicious torment, nearly fainting from the waves of pleasure she felt when he thrust her thighs apart and kissed her intimately. He was gentle but needful. He was leading her, directing her, but with pressing influence.

There was so much between them. Tracy knew this wasn't lust. The moments when she had relegated their relationship to one of lust skittered through Tracy's dazed mind. She'd been wrong. She was so moved by their lovemaking, and so was Slade. His caresses contained caring. Her every sense knew it.

He was very male, and every feminine instinct she possessed responded to his call. His mouth was skillful, a teasing coaxer, an intimate stimulator that gathered the hot liquid core of her into an explosive force, and the silence of the house was shattered by her cries.

Her thighs clasped around his head and she dug into his hair, racked by pulsing waves of pleasure so intense that she could only react physically.

Slade slid from her grasp, moved up beside her and enclosed her in a satisfied embrace. His lips stole over her hair, and her forehead, and his hand was at her breasts. She calmed slowly, shaken to her very soul. She hadn't expected what he'd done and was incredulous at the degree of pleasure she'd received from it.

But he still radiated desire. She felt his maleness, hard, throbbing, a hot reminder. She stirred, turned in his arms to face him. Her fingertips drifted boldly from his rib cage to his thighs, finally encircling his urgency. ''Tracy,'' he gasped, pulling her head to his chest. Her tongue flicked, tasting the saltiness of his skin.

There was a growl building in his throat. He moved swiftly, rolling her onto her back, and going with it, ending up on top of her. His eyes smoldered with a hot flame as he kneed her legs apart—not roughly, but not with as much gentleness as before. An odd thrill raced through her system, a sense of being mastered. She lifted her pelvis in invitation, met his murky gaze and took his penetration with a gasp.

Her thoughts became muddled as Slade whispered in her ear, "You mean too much to me...too much." It wasn't a lover's endearment; it was a hoarse, tortured cry.

It startled her, and she tried to stem the tide of his passion, but nothing could slow him, not words, not her feeble strength. She pushed against his shoulders, but to no avail. He was driven. His body was damp and wild.

Her eyes closed. She was breathing hard, her mind addled, her body responding despite her mental confusion. Her legs twined around him in a final consent. Her excitement crazed him further.

How she could do this, how she could eagerly allow this, was something she daren't think of or question. Nothing in her life had prepared her for such emotion, an emotion that filled her to capacity and could only spill out in an overflow of tears.

When it was over, when his body was limp and heavy on hers, when they were both spent and weak, she wept quietly, allowing the tears to drip from the

corners of her eyes to be absorbed by her hair and
the pillow.

Slade raised his head, frowned at the tears and
brushed them away with a thumb. "Why are you crying?"

Tracy turned her head.

"Look at me," he whispered, attempting to force
her gaze back with a gentle tug on her chin.

"The time!" She stared at the digital bedside
clock. It was almost time for Brock McFee to arrive.
"I've got to hurry, Slade. Let me get up." Her voice
was reedy, thin, betraying her emotional state.

He shook his head. "Not until you tell me why you
were crying."

"Why do you think?" The sharp question was followed immediately by remorse. "I'm sorry. Just let
me up, please."

He hesitated, watching her closely, wondering if he
had lost his mind. Yet he couldn't help saying, "What
if I wanted you to stay? Would you?"

"Stay!" The word was a gasp of disbelief. He'd
done everything but carry her to the airport. Now he
wanted her to stay?

"Do you even know what you want?" she finally
asked. "The helicopter will be here any minute. I've
got to fix my hair and…"

Passion gone, Slade's face registered a private rage
at life in general. She had to go. Of course she had
to go. What was wrong with him, even hinting he
wanted her to stay? Tracy's confusion was evident.

His wasn't so evident, but it was present, burning a hole in his gut.

He slid to the bed, his eyes dark with anger. It wasn't directed at Tracy. It was directed at the past— at Jason Moorland and, yes, even Jemma Dawson. Would he have to pay for their mistake his entire life? He'd paid as a child without a father, he'd paid as a teenager without a name, he'd paid every damned time it had come time to divvy up ranch profits, reminded over and over again that he owned only half of the Double J and that his very silent partner was a man he despised.

Now this, falling for Tracy Moorland. What a bitter, rotten joke, he thought.

He watched Tracy scurry from the room, heard her cross the hall to the bathroom, winced at the slam of the door. She would ready herself again and go. It would be over. No more need to skulk around, no more reason to stay away from the ranch.

It was what he had wanted from the day she'd arrived, and now that he was getting his "druthers", it hurt like hell.

He sighed mournfully and stood up. He was pulling his jeans on when he heard the bathroom door open.

Tracy came in, wrapped in a big white towel. Without looking at him, she began gathering up her clothes. The tears had dried on her face, but her eyes were bright. The tears were still very close.

He should have gone to Helena the minute he'd woken up. He shouldn't have taken her to bed again. Slade felt those truths so strongly that he ached with the knowledge. He knew she had feelings for him that he could never acknowledge or reciprocate. He should tell her the truth.

He advanced toward her. "Tracy—"

She recoiled. Her arms were full of her things, and she held them in front of herself like a shield. "No more, Slade," she pleaded huskily.

He drew a ragged breath. "I know. I just want to say something."

Tracy backed up and stopped beside a tall bureau. "I don't want to hear it," she replied weakly. She saw him take another step. Her gaze flickered to the door and back. "You've done enough," she whispered. "Just let me go in peace."

Then she looked at the top of the bureau. She asked herself a hundred times in the next few days what caused her to, but at the moment it was as though her eyes were drawn to the snapshot of their own accord. Perhaps the austerity of Slade's room had caused her to glance there. Nothing else occupied either of his dressers. They shone with polished emptiness, and the photo stood out. She was right next to it...and she looked at it.

Something zinged through her, a sense of recognition. Yet it wasn't really immediate recognition, it was more a feeling that she should recognize the man in the photo smiling up at her.

She frowned and shifted her load so she could hold it with one arm. Slade felt himself go pale when she picked up the picture and studied it.

Tracy frowned. It was an old black-and-white snapshot. The woman—the young, very pretty, smiling woman—looked a little like Slade. "Is...is she a relative?"

Slade felt choked. "My mother."

"And the man?" Even as she asked, she knew. It came to her later that she'd known even before she'd asked. The man in the picture was Jase, a young, very handsome Jase, with dark hair and snapping, intelligent eyes.

She lowered the picture slowly and faced Slade. "It's Jase, isn't it?"

Slade's face was a study in misery. It did no good to curse himself for leaving the photo out. With all that had happened, he'd simply forgotten. He nodded.

"Why was he with your mother?" She knew why, but she had to hear it from him, even though her skin crawled and her stomach lurched with nausea. But Slade wasn't answering. She could tell that. He was frozen with shock. And she hated him, she hated him so much she would gladly have destroyed him on the spot if there had been a way. "He was your father, wasn't he? Tell me, damn you! That's the secret you've been hiding, isn't it? Why?"

Her voice rose to a wounded wail. *"Why?"* Then it dropped to a barely audible "My God, why?" The snapshot fluttered to the floor from suddenly numb fingers. She had to get away. She whirled and ran.

Slade couldn't move. Numbness gripped him, too, but it held him in place for long, shattering minutes. Then, breathing resumed. He felt pain and so much remorse it staggered him. He had to talk to her, he had to help her through this.

Blindly he found his shirt and pulled it on, and then his socks and boots. He edged from the room, his heart pounding furiously, and stopped outside Tracy's closed door. Swallowing with difficulty, he rapped. "Tracy?"

There was no answer. "Tracy?" He knocked louder and tried the knob. The door was locked. "Open the door, Tracy."

He heard a weak "Leave me alone."

"No. Open the door."

Again there was no answer.

Slade stared at the door for a moment, then stepped back. He lunged, driving his shoulder against the solid wood. The old lock gave, and the door flew open.

Tracy never looked up. She was sitting on the bed, dry-eyed, nearly catatonic. Slade moved closer. "I think we should talk."

That only enraged her. "Now you want to talk?" Pure venom shot from her eyes. "What for? Do you think anything you could say could excuse what you've done?"

"Probably not. You have every right to be upset, but—"

"Upset!" Her bitter laugh was tinged with hysteria. "Upset hardly describes it." The enormity of the situation hit her again, and she covered her face with her hands. "Upset," she moaned. "Oh, God, that's almost funny."

Slade knelt down beside her and put his hands on

her arms. She jumped up and moved away in horror, clutching the towel around her. "Don't you dare touch me," she shouted. "Don't you ever touch me again!"

Slowly Slade stood up. "Will you listen a minute?"

"To what? Another lie?" Her face displayed her revulsion. "Do you know what you've done? Do you even know?"

His face grew hard. "Of course I know. I'm not completely insensitive."

"You're not? Well, it's a good thing you said so, because it sure isn't possible to detect from your actions." There was so much sarcasm and pain and anger in Tracy's voice that it sounded like someone else's.

The towel kept slipping, and she tugged at it again. "Get out of here so I can dress," she flung out coldly.

"I've seen you without clothes. Go ahead and dress. I'm not leaving."

"You smug bastard!" Her hands were shaking, but she managed to ball her clothes up, juggle them and the towel and head for the door at the same time.

Slade's voice stopped her. "I think you've summed it up pretty well."

"What?" She turned, understanding seeping into her befogged brain.

"That's exactly what I am. A bastard," Slade said harshly. "Your wonderful husband's bastard. But what does that make him? What kind of man would desert a pregnant woman and never even attempt to see his son? Think about that, Tracy. Give that a little thought.''

Now the questions formed. Dazed, Tracy battled the desire to know it all. She didn't want to talk to Slade Dawson. She wanted to put him from her life, from her mind. She wanted to get off the Double J and purge it from her memory.

But she knew she wouldn't be able to. She had made love with Jase's son! She had slept with her husband's son! Everything decent recoiled within her, every sense of morality, of right and wrong, of what was acceptable or unacceptable, was singed by the truth. Yes, she would think about it, and she didn't need Slade to belabor the point.

As if in a trance, she slowly turned away and walked to the bathroom, not even bothering to try the lock. It only worked half the time anyway, and if Slade wanted to intrude he would.

She dressed like an automaton, relying on habit and routine to button buttons and snap snaps. Clothed, she left the bathroom long enough to retrieve her cosmetic case, catching sight of Slade standing at the window in her room, obviously waiting for her. His back was all she could see, and his broad shoulders were slumped.

For a brief flash in time, she felt some of his pain. But she immediately squelched it. She had her own to deal with, and it was far worse than his.

Brushing angrily at the hot tears that suddenly filled her eyes, she returned to the bathroom, closing the door solidly.

Eight

He was glad she knew. Relief dislodged some of the ache, and Slade squared his shoulders. Now he could face Tracy with the truth of his burgeoning feelings for her.

Suddenly he realized that they didn't have much time. Not with McFee on his way to pick her up. Slade scanned the sky, searching the vacant blue for a sign of the helicopter.

Was it possible to make her understand how relieved he'd been that she hadn't known the dismal story? He'd hoped she would leave right away. If she had, that would have been the end of it. Each day she'd stayed had compounded his sin, inadvertently drawing Rachel and even Ben into the deception. Damn, it wasn't going to be easy. From Tracy's point of view, it appeared that the three of them had conspired to keep the truth from her, and it hadn't happened that way.

He heard the bathroom door open and heard the thud of the bag she replaced with the others in the hall. This was his only chance.

Slade crossed the room quickly and halted at the door. Tracy was ready, but her expression was ravaged. Neatness and a good makeup job couldn't conceal her red eyes or her tense body. She'd been crying, and Slade felt her pain in his soul.

"Will you talk to me?" he asked. His voice was steady, but his eyes were imploring.

She looked past him, as though she couldn't bear to see him. "Only because I need some answers."

"Whatever the reason, just talk to me." They were in the hall, standing, uneasy. The bedrooms were too intimate. "Let's go downstairs, all right?"

Tracy nodded reluctantly and reached for one of her suitcases. Hastily Slade moved to intercept her. "I'll do this. Go down and have some coffee. I'll just be a few minutes."

She could barely force a civil "Thank you." She wasn't merely upset, as he'd so cavalierly suggested; she was so deeply wounded that she wondered if she would ever recover.

Nevertheless, she preceded him down the stairs and went into the kitchen. The coffee was hot, but it had sat too long and was bitter in her mouth. She hadn't eaten a bite all day, and after the shocks of the past hour she felt ill. Trembling, Tracy poured a glass of milk, feeling its impact in her stomach gratefully. Milk had always soothed her, and it helped tremendously now.

Slade went up and down the stairs several times, finally appearing in the kitchen. "Everything's on the porch," he stated quietly.

"Thank you." It wasn't said very graciously, and she still couldn't make eye contact.

Spotting the half-empty glass in her hand, Slade asked. "Did you eat anything today?"

She tossed her head impatiently. "That's immaterial. I don't plan to discuss anything but one subject with you, Slade, only one. Why did you deem it necessary to lie to me? Why didn't you tell me the truth the day I got here?"

His voice was low. "I lied to you only one time, Tracy, when I told you I didn't know how Jason Moorland got involved with the ranch."

"I guess all that evasion and avoidance and outright rudeness doesn't count, does it? Well, excuse me if I don't see it that way. From the minute I set foot on this ranch, you've done nothing *but* lie."

"I did something else. I made love to you."

She nearly dropped the glass. "How dare you even mention that?" she said, her voice quavering. "I'll never forgive you. My God, you knew and you still—" She was trembling like a leaf in a windstorm, and she reached for the back of a chair for support.

Slade rushed forward and clasped her arm firmly. "Sit down," he commanded gruffly, steering her around the chair and seating her, even though she shrank from his touch. He pulled another chair away from the table and sat, too. "I'm going to tell you what I know. Yes, I should have done it right away. I can see that now. But I didn't."

With a shivering hand, Tracy brought the milk to her lips, seeking its comfort again. She wanted to hear this, but her senses recoiled at even being in the same room with Slade. Getting away from Slade and the ranch and Montana was the only desirable solution. Back in her own environment she could make sense of this.

But she'd never understand why Jase had deceived her, too. Why hadn't he told her he had a son? She had wanted a child so badly, and he had agreed a baby would be wonderful. But she had never conceived. She had been planning to take some fertility tests, had even discussed it with her doctor. But then Jase's heart attack had changed everything.

Tracy realized now that their childlessness hadn't been Jase's fault. The problem had to be with her.

But maybe she should be thankful. Slade had used no contraceptives, and she had certainly had had no reason to be on the pill before this. At least there was no danger now of being faced with an unwanted pregnancy, which was something she definitely had been remiss in not worrying about during the last two days.

In fact, it hadn't even crossed her mind, she realized weakly, remembering only how she hadn't been able to get enough of Slade, concerned about nothing but the blazing passion between them. Even now, hating him, she felt his pull, and she turned her hatred inward, despising her weakness for a man like him.

He was talking slowly, obviously dredging up painful memories. "He came to the valley thirty-three years ago. They fell in love. They were lovers."

Tracy pulled her thoughts together. "You learned that from your mother?"

"Yes. When she told him she was pregnant, he left. That's all there is to it, a few simple facts. But you and I are feeling the repercussions."

She withdrew from his attempt to ensnare her in the scenario. She wasn't a part of this. She never would be. "And the ranch?"

Slade stretched his long legs out in front of him and stared at his boots broodingly. "About a month after he left, Mother got a letter from an attorney. Jason Moorland had bought the ranch and put half of it in her name."

"And?"

"There's no 'and.' That's all I know. Except my mother's family didn't want her to take it and she defied them and took it anyway. She told me, when I was old enough, that she accepted it because of me. When she died I inherited her share—just like you did, Tracy. You and I became partners because of a terrible injustice more than thirty years ago. Ironic, isn't it?"

Tracy wasn't satisfied with the brief story. "Why did he leave your mother?"

Slade gave her a curious look. "I told you why. Because she was pregnant."

"Then why give her half this ranch? It had to be worth a small fortune, even thirty years ago."

Slade couldn't stop a bitter smirk. "Guilt. Why else?"

"Guilt." Tracy repeated dully. Yes, it could have been guilt. A man deserting a young woman carrying his child might try to assuage his guilt with something material. "But why not give her all of it?" Tracy asked thoughtfully, more to herself than Slade.

Slade lifted his eyebrows. "Good question, and one I never thought of before. Why did he retain half ownership?"

Realizing they were speaking much too chummily, Tracy drew herself up. "That's all. I have no more questions."

Slade's eyes narrowed. "Not even about me?"

"Especially about you." She got to her feet. "I'll wait outside."

Slade jumped up. "Just a minute!" He grabbed her shoulder and spun her around. "You can't leave just like that. What about us?"

"Us?" She was amazed. "There is no us."

"The hell there isn't."

"Are you crazy? I can't even bear the thought of what happened here. Do you actually think I would consider anything more between you and I?" She jerked her shoulder away from his hand.

"I care about you."

"Yes, I'm sure you do," she retorted sharply. "Just about as much as you would a—a prostitute."

"My God," he said, paling visibly. "Don't say things like that. I never thought of you that way."

"No? How *did* you think of me, Slade? Did you gloat over how eager I was to share your bed?" Her voice broke. "You are a bastard—and I'm not referring to your lineage, either. That's not your fault. You had nothing to do with the past. But you molded the present. You involved me in something so tasteless I'm ill from it. You're my deceased husband's son, for God's sake. What kind of woman would become knowingly involved—" She stopped at the sound of a helicopter. "He's here." Whirling, Tracy strode from the kitchen, Slade right behind her.

"Tracy, don't leave like this!"

Halting at the stack of luggage on the porch, Tracy turned. "I never want to see you again. Not ever! Do you understand?"

"I understand. Do you understand what you're doing? Something happened here, Tracy. I didn't want it to. Lord knows you weren't looking for it. But it happened nonetheless."

"Nothing happened here except some rather good sex. Do you wants thanks for it?"

Rather good sex? The comment wasn't in character. It was something he might have expected from some cheap tart, but not from Tracy. "You don't mean that," he said quietly. "You're only trying to hurt me."

"Think what you want. Isn't that what you told me earlier today?" God, had it only been today? It felt as if the day had been a thousand hours long. A sudden, terrible weariness overtook her. "Slade, that's enough. I can't take any more."

They both watched the helicopter settle down behind the trees. "In a few days—" Slade began helplessly.

"No. Not in a few days. Not in a few months."

He continued doggedly, "When you've had some time to digest all this, you'll feel differently. I know you will."

She turned and walked out the door.

For weeks Tracy walked around feeling almost as numb as she had after Jase's death. Her father noticed, at first attributing her abnormally fragile appearance to the rigors of travel. But when she didn't revert to her usual good health and spirits, he broached the subject at one of their Thursday lunches.

"Are you sure you're feeling all right?" Jim asked, deeply concerned about his only child. Even if she was close to thirty and independent as all get-out, Tracy was his world. Right now, picking at a delicious crab salad—a favorite dish of hers—she looked unwell.

"I'm fine, Dad. Just tired." It wasn't completely untrue. For some odd reason, she didn't seem able to get enough sleep. Of course, at least once each night she woke up to face again the horror of Jase and Slade being father and son. During the day it was easier to keep at bay, but without fail, she awoke at about two in the morning and relived every damn thing that had happened in Montana—including the times in Slade's bed. That was something she kept trying to forget, and she was relatively successful during daylight hours.

"Well, you look awfully peaked to me," Jim insisted. "If you don't perk up soon, I wish you'd see your doctor."

Tracy smiled, she hoped reassuringly. "Stop worrying, Dad. I'm as healthy as a horse," she declared, then winced. Why a horse, for crying out loud? Even her attempts at normal conversation were colored by memories of Slade. Horses, ranches, mountains...she didn't even want to think of them. Abruptly she changed the subject, and they finished lunch while chatting about a number of common interests.

Back at the Moorland Enterprises offices, Tracy had thrown herself into working up an in-depth report of her trip for the benefit of the three very capable accountants who kept track of the more mundane aspects of the estate. Kyle Wetherby, the head accountant, was loaded with questions about her stops, and she had decided to put her opinions and ideas on paper. It went well until she reached the Double J.

She had known in advance that it would bother her to describe the ranch, and she had tried to formulate an approach. She thought of Slade's offer to buy her interest, and the more she did, the more sensible it seemed. But she wanted no money. She wanted nothing but blessed forgetfulness. She wondered how she could handle the transaction without further complications.

While she wrestled with the problem, she received

a letter from Rachel. Tracy hadn't called, as she'd originally planned, sure that Slade would tell Rachel why she'd left. To curb her concern about Ben, Tracy had phoned the Helena hospital several times, gratified to learn that he was recovering nicely. Rachel's letter took her by surprise, and she was almost afraid to read it. But finally she opened it.

"Dear Tracy,
I hope you're all right. Slade told me everything, and I've debated writing, wondering if it was best to leave you be or let you know my feelings. Maybe the real reason I finally had to write is Jemma. I don't want you thinking she was a bad woman."

Tracy frowned. Jemma? Was that Slade's mother's name?

Of course! *J* for Jemma, *J* for Jase. That was how the ranch had gotten its name.

With a shudder, she resumed reading.

"Jemma was my best friend, and I probably knew her better than anyone, and she wasn't bad, Tracy. That's what I want you to understand. I keep wondering how Slade told you, just how he put it. Getting that out of him is impossible, as you well might know. He just keeps saying he told you the facts.

"Well, the facts sound very cold and heartless, don't they? I'm sure they were a terrible shock to you, especially when Slade also hinted at something personal between the two of you. I was worried about that, Tracy. I felt something in the air, an old woman's intuition, maybe. But I like you so much, and I didn't want you hurt.

"Slade either. I was so afraid he'd get hurt, and he's had his share of that. He's very unhappy, Tracy. He's always been a quiet man, but now he's even more quiet, sort of withdrawn. I wish with all my heart that he would have listened when I urged him to tell you the truth. It would have forestalled so much unhappiness. For the both of you.

"I will understand if you don't answer. But if you should take a notion, I would be thrilled to hear from you.

Your friend, Rachel Munley

P.S. Ben is doing good. He'll be in the hospital a few more weeks. They have him in some kind of traction because of his leg."

When Tracy put the letter down, her eyes were burning with unshed tears. She was having a hard enough time of it without hearing of Slade's "unhappiness." He should be unhappy! None of what had happened had been necessary. If he had been honest right away, they never would have gotten involved.

She drew a ragged breath. It was all his doing. If he hadn't kissed her on the balcony... *Why* did he kiss her on the balcony? He must have known how appalled she would have been if she had ever found out the truth. Yet he hadn't just kissed her, he had made love to her—beautiful, caring love.

It didn't help to remember that he had been nearly crazed with emotion during the last episode in his bed. His saying, "You mean too much to me," now made sense. If he had felt anything for her, he had tried to fight it. She couldn't negate that, no matter how hurt she was.

Sighing, Tracy put the letter away and wandered through the house. It was a gorgeous house, but it was so empty and lifeless. She didn't enjoy living here anymore. Quite the contrary, in fact. There were too many memories, too many sorrows associated with the house. She decided that she should sell it and find something more suited to her solitary life-style.

Sell the house, sell the ranch, get rid of everything connected with the past. Yes, that was best. It was time she made some much-needed decisions about her life. Perhaps even leaving San Francisco would help. A change of scenery might do a lot.

Where could she go? Someplace in the sun? Florida and Arizona were both possibilities. Of course, she would have to maintain contact with the office, but Kyle and the other two accountants did most of the real work. Her input consisted mostly of direction. It was her company, and her assistants awaited her decisions, but those could be handled long-distance.

Why not make a real change? she asked herself. Her father might be put out, but eventually he would accept her decision. She was ready to do something else, build a new life, perhaps even remarry someday.

That thought brought a piercing ache, and Tracy shied away from it. Like it or not, Slade Dawson held that particular spot in her heart. She couldn't construe what she felt for him as real love, not like what she'd felt for Jase. But there was no denying she had deep feelings for Slade, even if they were mixed with resentment.

That night she went to bed earlier than usual, trying to catch up on her sleep. She suspected her exhaustion had an emotional cause, for there was no doubt she'd been given an emotional drubbing. But it was so insistent, so debilitating. She gulped a handful of vitamins before crawling into bed, determined to shake the feeling.

She fell asleep fast and awoke with terrible nausea. Dashing for the bathroom, she was sick. Then she felt much better and returned to bed. It must have been those vitamins, she decided, planning to take them with meals from now on.

She never did answer Rachel's letter. Instead, she put her plan in motion, first discussing the sale of the ranch with Kyle. "I want you to take care of the necessary paperwork," she informed him. "Mr. Dawson expressed interest in buying me out, and I've decided to sell."

Kyle nodded agreeably. "I think it's a wise move. The ranch never did generate much profit."

"It's not profit I'm concerned with, Kyle. I just didn't like it." It was a lie, of course. She had loved the ranch.

"Did you come to an agreement on price?"

"No." Tracy lifted her eyes from a file folder she'd been toying with. "I don't want anything out of it."

Kyle was startled. "I don't understand."

"It's very simple. Give Mr. Dawson the ranch for one dollar. That will make it legal."

That bombshell was immediately followed by another. "I'm also going to sell my house and leave San Francisco."

"You're what?" Kyle Wetherby was a smallish man with horn-rimmed glasses, and he gave them a nervous push up his nose.

Tracy ignored the man's confusion. "Please find a good realtor to handle the house," she asked, and stood up. "Don't worry. I'll still take care of business. It's not necessary I be here every day, and I can fly here in a matter of hours should something come up." She smiled faintly. "We'll probably have a much larger phone bill, Kyle, but I have great faith in your ability to handle things."

Kyle rose slowly. "How soon do you plan to leave?"

"Probably not for several weeks. I have the house to deal with—or more accurately, what's *in* the house."

"Where are you going, Tracy?"

She sighed softly. "I'm not sure yet."

Clearly she had thrown the accountant for a loop, for he left her office shaking his head.

Her father wasn't going to be quite so easy to persuade, and if she dreaded anything in the mass of decisions she'd come to, it was telling him her plans.

Three times in the following week, Tracy woke up sick to her stomach within an hour of falling asleep. She couldn't figure it out. Apart from being more tired than she should have been, she felt well. Yet that insidious nausea kept dragging her from a deep sleep.

She kept telling herself it was just the aftermath of all she'd been through. Most of the time she was able to forget her discomfort until it returned.

The days passed swiftly. A group of realtors inspected and listed the house. Tracy knew the papers had been drawn up and mailed to Slade, and she got busy sorting and packing. Her father wasn't thrilled to learn that she was planning to leave San Francisco, and Tracy knew he felt she would change her mind before it actually came to pass.

Frankly, she wasn't sure he was wrong. She didn't really want to leave, because she didn't know where she wanted to go.

Montana, and the Double J, kept working their way into her brain every time she attempted real thought on the subject, and it was about to drive her up the wall. She was almost obsessed with the need to sever connections with the past, even with Jase. Yet all she could think of was Slade and the ranch. It made anyplace else very unattractive in comparison.

It surprised her that Slade didn't immediately sign and return the papers. When the time lag lengthened into weeks, she became extremely edgy. On top of that, her nocturnal nausea was getting worse. Tracy almost mentioned it to her father one day, but she backed off, knowing it would only worry him. It was beginning to worry her, too, and she decided to make an appointment to see her doctor.

She called and arranged a three-o'clock appointment for two days away, then settled down to work. Later in the day she called Kyle on the intercom, asking him to come to her office.

When he was seated, she got to the point. "Have you heard anything from Mr. Dawson?"

Kyle shook his head. "Not a word. One would think a man who'd been offered what you offered him would be jumping through hoops. What's with the guy? Is he some kind of weirdo?"

"He's not a weirdo," she said. "But he is different."

"Different enough to refuse a free ride?"

"What?"

Kyle shrugged. "Well, some people are too proud to take something for nothing. Did Slade Dawson strike you that way?"

Tracy frowned. Why hadn't that possibility occurred to her? "You may be right, Kyle."

"You might have insulted him, Tracy," Kyle said lightly, grinning at the incongruity of anyone being insulted by such a gift.

But Tracy took it seriously. She instantly realized the mistake she'd made and wondered in the next beat how to undo it. She didn't want direct contact with Slade, but perhaps a call from Kyle would help clear the air.

"Here's what I want you to do, Kyle. Call Mr.

Dawson and find out what he prefers. Accept anything he suggests. Just get the sale closed as quickly as possible.''

Kyle was long past his initial shock at Tracy ''giving'' valuable property away and agreed to handle it. A half hour later he stuck his head in the door and said, ''I tried to reach Mr. Dawson, Tracy, but he's away from the ranch.''

''Probably at Big Bluff,'' she murmured.

''Where?''

She shook her head. ''It's nowhere you'd know, Kyle. Whom did you speak to?''

''A lady. Rachel Munley. She said he'd be gone two or three days.''

''All right. Thank you. Try again at the end of the week.''

Shortly after lunch, feeling unusually out of sorts, Tracy went home. She was glad she'd made the doctor's appointment, because by the time she got home she was totally exhausted. The house was beginning to show signs of her intentions. Packing crates and cartons were scattered in several rooms.

She passed them all and went directly to her bedroom, kicked off her shoes and lay down with a weary sigh. Pulling the extra blanket she kept folded at the foot of the bed over herself, she dozed off without a bit of trouble.

For years Tracy had kept a three-day-a-week cleaning lady. Mildred Short wasn't really needed any longer, but Tracy hadn't had the heart to let her go yet, having grown very fond of the sharp-tongued woman. Mildred was busy in the kitchen when Tracy came home, but the older woman kept on with her chores, working around the packing cartons, clucking her tongue over her nebulous future.

She was ready to leave at her usual time, 4:00 p.m. She had made it nearly to the back door, handbag in hand, when the front door chimes rang out. Grunting impatiently, she changed directions. "Hold your horses," she commanded tartly as she wound through the house.

She pulled the door open. "Yes?"

A tall man in a dark, Western-cut suit stared at her. "I'd like to see Tracy Moorland. She lives here, doesn't she?"

"Well, of course she lives here. But she's resting."

"Could you tell her Slade Dawson is here, please?"

Mildred glared. "I'm not sure I should. Is she expecting you?"

"No, she's not. I just flew in. She didn't know I was coming."

An exasperated sigh lifted Mildred's bony shoulders. It was apparent to Slade that she wasn't thrilled to have to make a decision about the situation. "Well, wait here. I'll see what she says." Without ceremony, Mildred closed the door firmly.

She hurried down the hall and opened the door to Tracy's suite, frowning when she saw her snuggled under a blanket. She was about to close the door again when Tracy stirred.

"Mildred?" Tracy said sleepily. "Do you need me for something?"

Mildred sniffed. "There's someone here to see you. A man."

Tracy sat up and stretched. "Did he give you his name?"

"It's one of those funny names...Slade. Slade Dawson. Honestly, whatever happened to Joe or Pete? Do you know I have a friend whose daughter named her son Brighton? Did you ever hear of anything so silly? Brighton! What kind of a name is that for a boy to grow up with?"

Stunned, Tracy listened to Mildred's pungent commentary without moving. "Tell him I'll be right out." She got out of bed. "And Mildred, have him wait in the library."

Mildred raised a concerned eyebrow. "I was just leaving. Do you know him well enough to be alone in the house with him?"

"Yes. Don't worry. Mr. Dawson is an old friend."

The woman hurried away, and Tracy struggled to calm herself. Slade here? Why? This was something she had never visualized, and she wasn't sure how she felt about it. Yes, she had told him she never wanted to see him again, and maybe she should be angry.

But dear God, she wasn't a bit angry. She was weak with joy.

Nine

It had taken weeks for Slade to make the decision to visit Tracy. The sale agreement resided in his breast pocket, an ostensibly sound reason for making an appearance, but the truth of his visit was much more personal. A phone call wouldn't have been enough; he needed to see Tracy in person. Only by looking into her eyes would he know if she had come to terms with who he was.

Nothing had been the same after she'd left. She had entered his life like a tornado, and her departure had created a void he was having a hard time dealing with. He had to at least make an attempt to smooth the choppy waters.

The sale of the ranch offered a logical opportunity. He had been stunned to receive the papers, and even more stunned to read the terms. One dollar. He still couldn't believe Tracy thought he would take such an offer. Yes, he had always wanted total ownership. But he intended to pay a fair price for it.

He had talked to his banker, and a loan had been easy to arrange. The Double J was worth twice the amount he needed, and the richly collateralized loan was the type bankers were eager to make.

Slade waited for Tracy, looking outwardly cool, though inwardly he was a churning mass of uncertainty. The room exuded good taste and money, as did the other parts of the house he glimpsed. He was aware that this had been Jason Moorland's home, and it caused an uneasiness he couldn't dispel. Yet it was Tracy's home, too, and he tried to hang on to that thought as he surveyed the shelves of books, the posh furnishings.

He heard footsteps and stood up slowly, his eyes on the open door. Then she was there, framed in white woodwork, a vision that took his breath away. She was wearing blue again, a stylish blue dress, and he realized that in spite of her green eyes he liked her in blue better than in green. "Hello," he said softly.

"Hello, Slade." While Tracy hadn't managed to totally squelch the zinging of her blood at Mildred's announcement, she had succeeded in burying it beneath layers of composure. She knew she appeared quite calm, even under Slade's rather intense scrutiny.

Her chestnut hair was a swirl of glossy curls, and she was as beautiful as he remembered. Yet there was something subtly different about her face. He frowned, trying to pinpoint the change as she approached him. Her voice was the same, however, a husky melody that went right through him. "This is a surprise," she said, halting a safe distance away from him.

"I knew it would be." He couldn't stop staring. She was the same, and yet she wasn't the same. Maybe he shouldn't have come. Maybe the Tracy at the ranch and the Tracy in San Francisco were two different women.

She gestured with a graceful sweep of her hand. "Please sit down." She sank into a nearby chair.

"Thank you." He couldn't quite determine her reaction. In a puzzling way, they were strangers. His stomach cramped at the thought, his brain whirling with the memory of their interaction in Montana. She was too controlled, too reserved, and he feared her attitude hadn't changed at all. "I came about these," he announced quietly, extracting the papers from his coat pocket.

"Oh, the sale. Yes, I understand. I realized only today that you might have a problem with the offer." Tracy's aplomb concealed a heart that was hammering so hard she wondered it didn't raise the blue crepe of her dress bodice. He was so handsome, so utterly appealing in that dark gray suit and white shirt. She had never seen him in anything but jeans, she realized, and the suit was sharply creased, made from fine fabric and tailored in a perfect style for his broad shoulders and lithe body.

She continued. "I had one of my accountants call

the ranch this morning. He spoke to Rachel and she told him you would be gone a few days. We planned to call again at the end of the week.''

"About?''

''About the sale, of course. When you didn't return the papers… Well, it was quite apparent you weren't satisfied with the offer.''

"Did you really think I would take it?" Slade sat back and regarded her through curious gray eyes.

She lowered her gaze. "Perhaps I didn't give it enough thought.''

A silence stretched. Uncomfortable, Tracy looked up. "Let me get you something to drink.'' She rose. "What would you like?''

Slade stood too. "Whatever you have on hand.''

Lord, he was tall, so overwhelming, she thought. Just being in the same room with him made her feel softer and warmer than usual. It unnerved her and brought the tiniest quaver to her voice. "There's almost anything, Slade. Whatever you'd like.''

He nodded. "All right. Make it a Scotch and water.''

Feeling on tenterhooks, Tracy walked over to one of the bookshelves and pressed a button, and a section of the shelving slid open, revealing a well-stocked, lighted liquor cabinet. "I'll get some ice,'' she said, and hurried from the room.

Frowning, Slade approached the cabinet, studying the impressive array of bottles and crystal glasses. This was a different world from the Double J, no question about it. Maybe Tracy couldn't help being a different person here.

She returned with a silver ice bucket and began preparing Slade's drink. "Rachel didn't mention you were on your way to San Francisco," she said.

"Well, you know Rachel," Slade replied offhandedly.

Tracy stopped and looked up. "Yes. She doesn't offer information, does she?" For the first time, her gaze met his solidly. When she saw that he got her unspoken message, she broke eye contact, concentrating again on the drink. "Here you are." Their fingers brushed briefly while the glass was exchanged, creating a skittering tingle up Tracy's arm, and she grew even more nervous, but also more determined to hide it.

"Aren't you having anything?"

"Just some plain soda water." Tracy dropped ice cubes into a glass and filled it with soda. "My stomach has been acting up," she confessed. She was sorry the moment it was out. There was no reason to relate her discomfiture to Slade, and it set the wrong tone, sounded like a bid for a personal conversation. "Nothing serious, though," she added quickly.

"Tell me," she said, returning to her previous seat. "How is Ben doing?"

"He's hobbling around pretty well." Slade also ended up in the same chair he'd occupied before. "Grousing every step of the way, naturally. The doctor ordered him to stay off a horse for at least another month, and Ben's not overly thrilled about it."

Tracy smiled. "I can well imagine. And Rachel? Is she well?"

Slade nodded. "She's fine. Mothering Ben and loving every minute of it." He tried for a casual tone, but even he heard the strained note in his voice. They could both behave nonchalantly, but there was nothing nonchalant about the atmosphere in the room. "How have you been? Other than your stomach acting up, I mean?"

"Fine, fine," Tracy responded quickly, ignoring anything beyond the literal sense of his question. "Busy. I spend most days at the office. Usually I'm not home at this time of day."

"What brought you home today?"

Tracy realized that while they sat here and talked inanely she was making a furtive study, searching Slade for some similarity to Jase. "I wasn't feeling very well," she admitted absently, perplexed that she couldn't see any likeness.

"Bad stomach, not feeling well. Tracy, what's wrong? Have you seen a doctor?"

She colored, regretting having had another lapse. "It's nothing. Probably just nerves." Oh, hell, that hadn't helped. Now he was curious about her "nerves," probably surmising he was the cause of them. Well, he was, of course. But she didn't want to get into an involved discussion on that subject.

The sale! It was a safe topic. "If you're going to be in town a few days, you could come to the office and arrange the terms of the sale to your liking. Kyle Wetherby is handling it for me."

"Not you?"

"No. Kyle is my right-hand man, a very competent accountant. He worked with the attorneys on the original papers."

Slade sipped his Scotch, eyeing her over the glass. "Accountants, attorneys—sounds like you're right in the thick of big business. Do you enjoy it?"

"Well, sometimes I do. Actually, my contribution consists mainly of overseeing financial reports."

"Counting your money, so to speak?"

A rush of pink stained Tracy's cheeks. "Did I sound that patronizing?"

Slade smiled. "Not really. I'm just trying to adapt that image to the woman who suddenly dropped out of the sky one day. It's hard to do," he added quietly.

That flustered her. "I shouldn't have arrived so dramatically. A car would have been better."

"Maybe. But then, the method of your arrival wasn't really the problem, was it?"

"No, I guess not." She drew a quick breath. "Well, we've covered Ben and Rachel and me. That leaves you. How have you been?"

His eyes narrowed. "Do you really want to know?"

She veered away from the main theme. "Have you been to Big Bluff lately?"

"A few times. Making sure everything is ready for hunting season, mostly. About six or seven friends will be using the cabin in the next few weeks."

"To get their deer?"

"And elk."

Just like that, they ran out of small talk. Tracy sipped her soda water nervously, watching Slade do the same with his drink. Why had he come? The sale modifications could have been handled just as well by phone. She tried to sort out her feelings, and it was hard to do.

She was confused. She felt him in every pore, in every cell, not wanting to, worrying why he didn't resemble Jase at least a little. She kept wishing he would go, hoping he wouldn't.

Slade broke the heavy silence. "How about dinner together?"

The suggestion startled her. "Dinner?"

"Yes. I don't know my way around very well, but you must know a nice place."

"Well, I'm not sure—"

"Do you have other plans?"

She hesitated. This was silly. They were both skirting the issue, avoiding the obvious. "That's not a good idea, Slade," she said softly.

He studied her for a long moment. "You still can't deal with it, can you?"

Her voice broke. "No. I'm sorry. I can't."

He sounded exasperated and empty. "Will you ever be able to?"

"I don't know." It was said simply, and it was a true assessment of her state of mind.

Slade tossed back the rest of his drink and set the glass on the coffee table. "You're wrong, you know. You're blaming you and me for something that happened a long time ago."

"I'm blaming you, Slade," she retorted instantly. "I won't take any responsibility for what happened, not thirty years ago, not last summer. Oh, you had no more to do with the past than I did, but you had everything to do with what happened last summer."

His eyes were dark and piercing. "Do you really regret it so much? Have you been able to forget? I haven't. I think of you all the time."

Her wince was visible. "I don't want to hear it. If you've suffered, well, so have I. But I won't compound our mistake."

"And dinner together would compound it?"

She met his gaze. "It might."

His smile was partly sardonic, partly poignant. "Because you know damn well there's something between us."

"There was," she admitted. "But it's over. It was over the minute I saw that picture." Damn, the pain of that moment was so easily revived. She felt it now, in her heart, in her mind, and it was unfair. He had no right to remind her.

He had never been loquacious, and he had often envied the gift of gab some of his friends had. He only knew how to say what he felt, and he didn't want to leave without doing so. But a simple "I think I'm in love with you," might send her into a tizzy. She was too tense. In spite of the control she cloaked herself with, he sensed her underlying distress.

"You mean a great deal to me, Tracy," he stated without fanfare, yet with enough emotion to touch on a deeper meaning than the mere words implied.

She felt astonished. How dare he burden her with this? She actually stopped breathing for a moment, then gulped in a lungful of air. Too edgy to sit still, she stood up. Her face was pale, her voice unsteady. "Don't say things like that. I won't listen, Slade. You have no right—"

"No right?" He got to his feet. "I need a 'right' to care about you? Where do I get it? How do I get it? Is it a permit or a license? Tell me what to do, Tracy. I'll do it."

"Don't be silly," she whispered.

"I'm not trying to be. I'm deadly serious. Tell me what you want me to do and I'll do it. Only, dammit, don't close the door." While he spoke, he advanced, and he ended up very close to her, close enough to catch her scent. "Tracy—"

"No!" She stepped aside, uncomfortable with his nearness. "This is why you came, isn't it? To badger me? How could you think anything had changed? You're still his son. In ten years you'll still be his son, in fifty years. There is nothing you or anybody else can do to change that."

"Then why try?" Slade was rapidly approaching anger. He knew it was impossible to change hard facts, but in the long run, did his parentage really matter?

The anger drained away. Hell, yes, it mattered. It mattered as much to him as it did to Tracy. How could he blame her for taking a righteous stand when he was ravaged by the same torment?

"I think that should have been my line, don't you?

I'm not the one trying, Slade, you are." Her retreat had taken her across the room, and from that safe distance she faced him. "I won't belabor this thing, Slade. Not again."

"We hardly talked about it before," he said sharply.

"That wasn't my fault, either. You had a hundred opportunities, and you eluded every one of them. If I hadn't seen that snapshot I still wouldn't know, would I? You were going to let me leave without a word. Then what, Slade? Did you think I'd come back here and just put everything out of my mind?" The enormity of such a possibility struck her. "My Lord, how did you envision the aftermath of my visit?"

Slade knew he had to be honest. This was no time for dancing around the truth. "I didn't. I'm not trying to excuse what I did. But try to realize I didn't expect what happened any more than you did."

She pinned him with a hard-eyed look. "Maybe what I can't forgive is that final day. The first time in your bed is almost acceptable. I think it took us both by surprise. But not the next day, Slade. You deliberately made love to me."

"I won't deny it. I couldn't stop myself. I was discovering—"

"Don't say any more! I wish you'd go." Her hands were clasped together, her eyes haunted. "You shouldn't have come here."

Slade felt anger burning his gut. He was facing a brick wall, and he had hoped for so much. "You won't even make a stab at forgiving me, will you?"

It occurred to her in a blinding flash that he thought that was the crux of the matter. "Forgiveness isn't going to suddenly make you another man's son," she cried.

He was powerless against that argument, and for a time, while he stared at her and suffered the agony of events beyond his control, all the hatred he'd grown up with for Jason Moorland returned tenfold. The man was a ghostly intruder. He still influenced Slade's life, even from the grave.

Bitterness altered his expression, and crept into his eyes. "You're right," he growled. "Forgiveness wouldn't change a damn thing, would it?"

Slade turned to the door. Tracy watched him go, very close to bursting into tears. Then he stopped and gave her one last heated look. "Take care of yourself. You don't look well."

The next moment, he was gone. At the slam of the front door, Tracy ran to the foyer and peeked through the blinds. The driveway was empty. He must have arrived by taxi. She watched his long-legged stride carry him to the street. She wanted to run out and call to him, to offer him a ride or the use of the telephone.

But she did nothing, knowing it was best that they spend no more time together. And when he was out of sight, she dropped the blind and turned away. She was sick at heart, and she knew exactly why she felt as if the world had just come to an end. She loved him, this rugged Montanan, with a fierce intensity that surpassed any emotion she had ever possessed.

No, it wasn't like what she had known for Jase.

She shouldn't have tried to compare two such vastly different feelings. Jase had evoked a serene affection; Slade awoke passion and excitement and life. Just having him in the house had caused the air to vibrate, and she could still feel it.

Suddenly the silence of the house was unbearable. She couldn't stand it, couldn't face the lonely evening ahead, and with unaccustomed haste she ran to the phone and dialed her father's office number. "Dad?"

"Tracy? Is something wrong?"

She had spoken too breathlessly, too anxiously, giving away her distraught mood. "No, no, nothing's wrong. I—I was just wondering if you'd like to have dinner with me."

"Honey, I'm sorry, I've already made plans. Maybe tomorrow night?"

"Oh. Well…"

"Tracy, are you sure nothing's wrong? You sound upset."

She felt like a tightly coiled spring. "Nothing's wrong, Dad. I'm fine. Really."

"Well, if you're sure."

Somehow she convinced her father, but after hanging up she prowled the house restlessly. Where was Slade staying? Would he come to the office tomorrow and complete the sale?

Was he hurting as bad as she was?

What would he have said if she hadn't stopped him?

The insistent questions hounded her so cruelly that

she knew she had to stop dwelling on them. The only way to accomplish that was to do something.

With that in mind, Tracy changed into a pair of old jeans and a T-shirt and dived into some more packing. She made the library her assignment and carried a dozen strong cartons into that room.

By ten the shelves were stripped and the cartons taped shut and labeled. She stood up and brushed some hair back from her forehead wearily. A bowl of soup, a warm bath and bed sounded good.

She had made it through the evening. Just as she could make it through tomorrow evening and the evening after that.

"And on and on into the future," she whispered, overwhelmed by a feeling of emptiness. But it was all she could foresee at the present.

All she could do was hope things would change once she made her planned break with the past.

Tracy had been on pins and needles, thinking Slade might suddenly show up at the office. He didn't, nor did he call. She had given up all hope of hearing from him. But two days after her assault on the library, Kyle came into her office. "Just had a call from the elusive Mr. Dawson." He grinned.

Tracy's pulse leaped. "And?"

"Evidently he got back home and—"

"You mean he called from the ranch?"

"Right. He's one head-on guy, isn't he?"

Tracy felt deflated. Slade had gone back to Montana without taking care of the sale, let alone making another attempt to see her. "What did he say?" she asked dully.

Kyle shook his head, displaying mild amazement. "He laid it out, exactly how he wanted the sale handled—one, two, three. Like I said, head-on. By the way, the price he quoted is very fair."

Who cares? she wanted to say. Money was the farthest thing from her mind. She already had more money than she could spend in three lifetimes, and a fat lot of happiness it had bought her. "That's good," she responded listlessly. "You can finalize the deal, Kyle. Frankly, I'd just as soon not hear another word about it."

Kyle looked perplexed, but he got up with a shrug. "No problem. I'll take care of everything."

"Thank you. And Kyle, please close the door on your way out," she called as the accountant strolled from the room.

Alone, Tracy turned her chair so that she could look out the window behind her desk. The view was wonderful, one she often derived pleasure from. But today the tears in her eyes blurred Golden Gate Bridge and the bay, and she saw none of the distant ships and sailboats kicking up waves in the dark water.

Slade had completely accepted her stand, and it was ridiculous to be upset over something she had demanded. Yet now she realized how much she had counted on seeing him again, even if only for business purposes.

It was truly over, and she wouldn't see the Double

J's name on financial reports anymore. She had succeeded in cutting the ties, in making a total break.

She had never been more miserable in her entire life.

A few days later, Tracy hurried into the office of Dr. Maynard Lessing. The kindly, older man was seated at his desk, and he looked up from Tracy's chart. "Have a chair."

"Thank you." She sat down. "Well, anything I should be worried about?" Tracy had finally broken down and gone to her doctor. She couldn't understand why she felt so run-down all the time.

Dr. Lessing placed his elbows on the desk and made a tent of his fingertips. "This could be delicate. I think it best to just be frank. Tracy, I think you're pregnant."

She stared. She felt light-headed, and she could barely breathe. "Pregnant?" she echoed feebly.

"I'd like to take a few tests, but I feel fairly certain of the results. You're not far along. Two months at the most." His voice grew very gentle. "It is possible, isn't it?"

Dr. Lessing knew perfectly well she was a widow, and she could tell he was trying to remain impassive. But a spark of curiosity was in the air just the same.

She nodded weakly. "It's possible," she whispered. "But I...I thought it was impossible. I mean, in four years of marriage I never conceived."

"It might not have been your fault," Dr. Lessing said gently.

Her eyes widened. "Oh, it couldn't have been Jase's fault. He—" She stopped herself from blurting out the facts. "Maybe it's something else," she suggested hopefully. "I've heard a lot about morning sickness, but night sickness?"

"Quite common," Dr. Lessing replied. He sat back, viewing his patient's distress. "Nothing says you have to sustain this pregnancy, Tracy. I'm not suggesting anything, because it's entirely your decision, but at this stage abortion is a very simple procedure."

Tracy was shocked. Abortion? When she had always wanted a baby so much? My God, this was Slade's baby. She would never harm an unborn life, especially when she knew she was in love with its father. She shook her head vigorously, refusing even to consider the horrifying suggestion. "No," she declared vehemently. "Never, Dr. Lessing."

"Then you're not unhappy about this?"

"I'm stunned," she confessed, still too shaken to speak steadily. "But unhappy?" A sudden, piercing joy rocketed through her, and she smiled. "No, I'm not unhappy. I'm not sure what I am, but it's not unhappy."

Dr. Lessing released a relieved breath. "I'm very glad. It's my duty to point out alternatives, but I'm always delighted when a woman is happy over a baby." He stood up. "See my secretary before you leave and make another appointment, and call me tomorrow afternoon for the results of the test. Like I said, I'm quite certain, but there's always that odd chance.''

Tracy rose slowly, picking up her handbag with studied concentration. She was busy assimilating the news, and her mind alternately raced and slowed down. A baby. An honest-to-goodness baby. It was a miracle, and a problem—maybe many problems. But a baby!

She couldn't stop smiling. She offered the doctor her hand. ''Thank you, Doctor, thank you very much.''

Dr. Lessing beamed, holding her hand in both of his. ''You didn't need those fertility tests we spoke of at all, did you? It was no doubt a problem with Mr. Moorland, Tracy.''

Her smile faded. If it hadn't been her fault—and it hadn't been Jase's fault—why hadn't she become pregnant during her marriage?

Ten

A thought she couldn't quite formulate gnawed at Tracy for the rest of the day. While she was getting ready for bed that night, it came together. "What if Slade *isn't* Jase's son!" she exclaimed aloud.

A wild hope brought a dizzying energy and, half-clothed, Tracy paced around the bedroom. It explained several different points—her presumed infertility, of course, and also why Slade didn't bear the slightest resemblance to Jase.

Of course, that wasn't one hundred percent true. Hadn't she bemoaned their similarity as far as their exaggerated need for privacy went? Yet that was such an intangible likeness, a characteristic many people exhibited and certainly not enough to irrevocably tie the two men together.

There was more to Jemma and Jase's past than Slade had related, Tracy realized, wondering at once if he had kept something back. With all his secretiveness and evasion, that was entirely possible. In the next instant, she doubted Slade knew any more than he'd stated. She recalled that once she'd seen the old photo he had actually seemed relieved.

But Rachel knew the truth.

Excitement made Tracy's pulse leap, and she ran to find Rachel's letter. It took several minutes, but she finally located it in a desk drawer in the library. Quickly she reread it, lingering over the words Rachel had written. *Jemma was my best friend, and I probably knew her better than anyone, and she wasn't bad, Tracy.*

Why had Rachel surmised she would think Jemma a bad woman? Of course, the phrase was old-fashioned, but it effectively conveyed Rachel's fears.

When she had received the letter, she hadn't tried to read between the lines, Tracy realized. But Rachel's defensiveness now looked odd. What did it matter what she might think of Jemma Dawson? Actually, she had given very little thought to Jemma one way or the other. It wasn't that poor, sad woman who had broken her heart in Montana; it was her son.

Sighing, Tracy put the letter away. Would Rachel ever admit the truth? she wondered.

Tracy realized that Rachel Munley's loyalty to Jemma was a steadfast reality. Tracy had had plenty of experience with it during her week on the ranch, and she knew Rachel wouldn't bare her soul without a very good reason.

Tracy's hands went to her abdomen, and the marvel of the baby washed over her again. Would a child be reason enough? Would Slade's baby loosen Rachel's tongue?

She couldn't chance it. As things stood, Tracy was afraid to attempt to pry the old story out of the woman. She hadn't completely decided whether or not to let Slade know about the baby, but she was leaning towards *not* telling him. Even though her love for him made her feel guilty about that decision, she couldn't face all the problems that would arise if he knew she was carrying his child. He would want some say in the child's welfare, its rearing. But most importantly, it would forever cement Slade and her together in a way she couldn't bear.

She was horribly torn, ecstatically happy, deeply despondent. This was the most wonderful thing that had ever happened to her, but at a time when she should be wild with joyful satisfaction, she was sadly divided, unable even to share the incredible news with her father.

Jim Kirkland would ask questions. He would wonder who the father was. He'd probably be angry with her when she refused to tell him. No, she couldn't put either her father or herself through that. She would do as she'd planned, she decided, recognizing the timeliness of her decision to leave San Francisco.

In time she could concoct a story to explain the child. Perhaps she would tell the truth with a fictionalized man in Slade's role, perhaps she would pretend she had adopted. At least, happily, she had something very real to look forward to now. A child made all the difference.

Slade's child.

Tracy crumpled and lowered her head to her arms on the desk, pain creating a spasm of bitter tears. She loved him. She should be on the phone right now, calling him, telling him she loved him and that they were going to have a child.

Oh, it was all too much. Tracy dragged herself from the chair and returned to her bedroom. She finished getting ready for bed, forcing her thoughts away from Slade. It was time to do more than halfheartedly think of the future; it was time to get on with it.

In the weeks that followed, Tracy went through the house methodically, enlisting Mildred's aid in carefully packing crystal and china. It wasn't until she reached Jase's personal dressing room and closet that she realized she had put that task off until last. Everything was exactly as he had left it, the rows of suits, the stacks of shirts and sweaters, all his clothing. She hadn't wanted to deal with this chore since his death, and the door to the large room had remained firmly closed for a year and a half.

Even now, she approached the job with trepidation, knowing she should have done this long ago, still uneasy about it. Even now she felt as if she were invading the privacy Jase had so steadfastly guarded. Perhaps that was why she had avoided it.

Well, it couldn't be avoided any longer, Tracy realized as she stepped through the door to survey the neat array of clothing. Someone could use all these garments. She would give them to a charitable organization.

One by one Tracy removed expensive suits from hangers, folded them and laid them in cartons. Then sport coats, slacks, shirts, sweaters, drawers of underwear and socks. She filled two whole cartons of shoes. She yanked at another drawer, expecting it to slide open immediately as the others had done, and was surprised when it didn't.

It was locked.

Frowning, Tracy straightened and stared at the stubborn drawer. Why would Jase have a locked drawer in his closet?

She remembered his key ring and wondered where she had put it.

Ah, yes, she recalled. His leather jewelry case.

In minutes she was back with the keys, and after trying a few she found the right one. The lock clicked, and she pulled the drawer open.

She sank to the floor to examine the contents, a small, neatly banded-together bundle of papers and a stack of plainly bound books.

And a snapshot. The same one Slade had.

Tracy's mouth dropped open, and her fingers shook as she pulled the rubber band from the packet. There were letters, which she set aside for the moment, and an official-looking document. She unfolded it and saw a copy of the deed to the ranch, whereby ''Jason F.

Moorland conveyed to Jemma L. Dawson half interest in that certain property, described as…''

She put the paper down and reached for the letters, her brain on fire with what she had stumbled upon. There were three letters, and she read them with her heart pounding and tears blurring the words. Then she wearily sat back against the closed drawers. It was all true. Jemma had related her pregnancy, pleading for Jase's understanding. Three times she had tried, and from what the letters revealed, she had repeatedly failed.

Tracy eyed the books fearfully. Their bindings were various colors, some of them rather faded with age. What were they?

Feeling as though the wind had been knocked out of her, she removed the top book from the drawer and opened it. Jase's precise handwriting leaped out at her. A journal? A personal journal?

Yes. That was what it was, an almost daily record of Jase's life.

She flipped pages, reading about the events of the last year before Jase's death. She was in it, her name appeared often, and it wasn't merely a factual accounting of Jase's activities. He had set his thoughts down, too.

She was in a state of shock, and she went flipping pages wildly, stopping to read a paragraph, then rushing to another page. It was all there, their entire four years together. She couldn't believe it, and she felt rather queasy.

One by one she took the journals from the drawer

and traced Jason Moorland's life. But she couldn't bear reading all the details and skipped book after book. She knew she would find Jemma in one of the older volumes, and she searched for the one that would recount that period of Jase's life.

Then she found it, a complete history of how he had gone to the valley in search of land, how he had met Jemma Dawson, "a lovely young woman with long black hair and radiant blue eyes." He was almost poetic in his description of Jemma, revealing a deep emotional involvement.

Tracy could hardly breathe. How had she lived with a man four years and not known his compulsion to keep records? Jase had even jotted down weather statistics. She learned that the day he had met Jemma Dawson the sun had been shining and the temperature had been a perfect seventy-eight degrees.

Then there were pages of intense emotion. "I love her, I love her with a passion that amazes me. I am going to ask her to marry me. She is everything I want in a wife, beautiful, intelligent, full of life." But if he *had* loved Jemma, why had he left her?

She read on and nearly fainted. "I've decided not to tell her of my sterility. It isn't important. A child would come between us anyway. I want only her."

Stunned, Tracy grappled with the pile of books at her feet, searching again for the latest journal. Breathing hard, as though she'd just run a footrace, she found the pages recounting her early relationship with Jase.

There it was, another reference to his "sterility."

"Tracy is young and will probably want children. I'm afraid if I tell her of my sterility she will back away from me, which I couldn't bear. I will remain silent on the subject."

Tracy ran her fingers through her hair. What a tragic, unnecessary horror Jase had put her through. He wasn't Slade's father. He wasn't anyone's father.

But who *was* Slade's father?

She returned to the older journal, wincing at the bitterness that suddenly appeared. "The fool, actually trying to convince me I'm the father of her bastard. She has ruined everything. We could have had so much together."

Then, several pages later: "Lord help me, I still love her. I cannot get past it, no matter how I try. I suspect I always will. And she has nothing, no way to take care of herself and the child. She has written, and her parents are condemning, cruel. I must help her."

"Thus the ranch," Tracy mumbled thickly, closing the journal.

Her stomach churned so violently that she was sure she was going to be sick, and she left the dressing room and went to her bathroom to gulp a mouthful of the liquid antacid Dr. Lessing had prescribed.

She went to the bedroom, the packing forgotten. Lying on the bed, she stared unseeingly at the ceiling. So it had all been a lie. Why, for God's sake? Why had Jemma told her son such a terrible, far-reaching lie?

Tracy realized that Rachel knew why Jemma had

raised Slade to believe Jason Moorland was his father. And now Tracy had the evidence to confront Rachel with. Even the staunch housekeeper couldn't stay silent with Jase's journals in front of her.

Slade would have to believe, too, wouldn't he? To think he had despised a man his whole life who hadn't deserved such rancor brought tears to Tracy's eyes. What a terrible waste. Poor Jase, the unwitting recipient of such misplaced hatred. His worst crime had been worrying about a woman he'd truly loved. If it hadn't been for Jase's concern, Slade wouldn't have the ranch he loved so much. He had to learn the truth.

With that behind them, could she tell him about the baby?

Tracy's heart ached. What she really wanted was to share her happiness over the baby with Slade, to tell him she loved him and hear that he loved her, too.

If he did.

He cared about her. Wasn't that what he had said? But was that the kind of love that would endure and provide a strong foundation for the three of them: Slade, herself, the baby?

Interspersed with that concern was another. Knowing she loved Slade Dawson didn't preclude a few reservations. There was still the question of knowing each other well enough for a permanent relationship. Being in love with a taciturn man wasn't a simple matter. What did she really know of Slade, apart from his sexual charisma? Had they ever really talked, freely exchanged ideas and opinions?

In fact, they had never once sat down to a meal together. It was ironic that during his brief visit to her house he'd asked her to dinner, when, in Montana, he'd done everything possible to avoid eating with her.

There were too many unknowns for her to just shove her fears aside casually. But she couldn't set the other things aside, either, her deeply felt emotional ties to Slade, the wonderful uninhibited passion he brought to life.

But first things first, Tracy decided. Speaking to Rachel was crucial. Tracy didn't want to risk transferring Slade's hatred from Jase to Jemma. He revered his mother, and it was important to maintain that love. Tarnishing Jemma's memory might damage her son in a way he might never get over. That was something Tracy wouldn't do, even if it meant her own unhappiness.

No, she had to talk to Rachel before she ever saw Slade. Only then could she work on the other aspects of the relationship. Rachel couldn't deny the journals, and only she could provide the rest of the story. There were still gaps, even with Jase's precise record, and only after hearing the rest could Tracy make an intelligent decision about Slade. Everything rested on Jemma's side of the story, Tracy realized, and that was something she could only get from Rachel.

Within a week, Tracy had pulled herself together enough to place a call to the ranch. As Tracy had suspected she would, Rachel answered the phone. "Hello, Rachel. This is Tracy Moorland."

"Tracy! How nice to hear your voice. How are you, honey?"

"Very well, thank you, Rachel. I need to see you."

"Me? Well, you know where to find me," Rachel quipped, laughing lightly.

"Yes, but I want to talk to you away from the ranch. I'm flying to Helena in the morning. My plane gets in at 11:30. I know it's a long ride, but could you meet it, please?"

"Well, yes, I suppose I could."

Tracy detected the sudden caution in Rachel's voice. "Thank you. I'd just as soon keep this between you and me. Please don't say anything to Slade."

"I couldn't if I wanted to. He's up at Big Bluff."

"Is it still hunting season there?"

"The tail end. Slade won't be back for a few more days."

"I see. Well, that eliminates you making excuses for the trip to Helena."

"Tracy, what's this all about?"

"Jase and Jemma," Tracy replied softly, and heard Rachel's stunned intake of air.

"I'm not going to discuss that with you," Rachel said stubbornly.

"I think you will, Rachel. You see, I found an old journal of Jase's. I want to show it to you."

A choked "My Lord" came over the line. Then: "Well, all right. I'll see you tomorrow."

* * *

Montana was cold, and there were several inches of snow on the ground. Tracy had packed a suitcase full of warm clothing, and was bundled up in a heavy coat, a scarf, gloves and a knit hat. She viewed the winter scenery with enthusiasm while Rachel drove them to a restaurant for lunch. Neither had mentioned Jase or Jemma yet, and Tracy was determined to refrain until they were comfortably seated in the nice place Rachel had told her about.

The "Westwind" was as nice as Rachel had promised. They ordered lunch and received a steaming pot of hot herbal tea to drink while their food was being prepared, and finally Tracy met Rachel's inquisitive eyes. Without further ado, she drew the journal from her shoulder bag and thrust it across the table. "I've marked the pages to read with paper clips," she said quietly, turning to her tea while Rachel read.

There was anguish in the older woman's face when she lifted her eyes from the book. "Where did you get this?"

"I've been going through everything in the house, Rachel. I'm planning to leave San Francisco. Finally, after all this time, I went through Jase's dressing room. That book, and about eight others, were in a locked drawer."

Rachel was pale. "You're not going to show this to Slade, are you?"

"That depends on you, Rachel."

"On me? Why on me?"

"Because you're the only one who knows the complete story." Tracy regarded Rachel sympathetically.

"I know how loyal you've been. But this is so very important. I have to know everything."

"Why do you have to know? It's none of your business!"

"Oh, but it is." She stopped, formulated her thoughts and went on. "Slade is not Jase's son. We both know that. I want Slade to know it, too. He's wasted his life hating a man who did him no harm, although Jemma must have had a reason for lying. I guess what I'm saying is, it really depends on that reason whether I go directly to Slade or catch the next plane back to San Francisco."

Rachel thought about that, and resentment suddenly flared in her face. "Why don't you just leave him alone?"

"Because I love him, Rachel. But I love him enough to leave him alone if I think he will be more hurt by the truth than by those abominable lies he's living with. Didn't you get tired of lies? How could you have been a party to such deception?"

Tears suddenly filled Rachel's eyes. Seemingly embarrassed, she fished a tissue from her purse and dabbed at them. "Of course I got tired of it. It was awful. After Jemma died, I almost told Slade the truth, but I had promised Jemma, I promised her so long ago. How could I go back on that? She was more like a sister than a friend. Besides, it was too late. If you tell Slade now, he'll hate me. Is that what you want?"

"Of course not. I don't want him hating anyone. That's what I've been worried about. Rachel, what happened thirty years ago? I'm not going to hurt Slade. Believe me, if I'd been going to do anything impulsive, I would have called him, not you.''

Rachel sniffed and nodded. ''I suppose so.'' She blew her nose, sipped her tea and at long last regarded Tracy with relative calm. ''Jason Moorland came to the valley one summer. He just showed up, and I think he was looking for a ranch to buy, because it got around that he was talking to several different ranchers about their places.''

That fit in with the journal's information, and Tracy nodded. ''Go on.''

Rachel looked chagrined. ''Before he got here, Jemma had been involved with—'' she seemed to choke on the name ''—with Garve Hutchins.''

Tracy's heart skipped a beat. ''Is he Slade's father?''

Rachel nodded unhappily. ''Yes. To go back even farther, I'd like to tell you a little about Jemma. She was the prettiest girl in the valley. We were thick as thieves, the kind of friends who tell each other everything. We shared our first crushes on the skinny little boys in fifth grade, and our first kisses as we got older.

''During high school, Jemma dated a dozen different boys. She was the most popular girl in school. But she was a *good* girl,'' Rachel said fiercely. ''Sex wasn't taken lightly in those days, Tracy. Oh, the boys weren't any different than they are now, I'm sure. But we girls were. We talked about sex, we wondered about it, we read everything we could get our hands on that even hinted of sex, but very few of us experienced it.''

Rachel stopped long enough to bring her teacup to her lips. ''We were seniors when Jemma met Garve Hutchins. I met him, too, of course, everyone did. He was older, out of school, and the new kid on the block, I guess you could say. Why his family ever moved here I'll never know, but they were dirt-poor, a trashy bunch, and lived in a little shack on one of the ranches in the valley. Garve went to work as a cowhand, and he probably didn't earn much, but it was enough to afford him an old car and a few pairs of tight jeans.''

Tracy registered Rachel's repugnance and sighed, foreseeing what was coming.

''Jemma just went crazy for him. Garve was a handsome devil, I'll give him that—black wavy hair, an arrogant face, a swagger in his walk. The only problem was, he was peacock-conceited and didn't have a lick of sense. Neither did Jemma where he was concerned.''

Rachel's expression grew distant as she went back in time. ''She never stopped confiding in me, and I was half-crazy worrying about what they were doing. I told her she'd get caught—that's the old term for pregnant. In those days a girl didn't get pregnant, she got 'caught.'

''Well, she wouldn't listen to me. She kept saying they were in love. Love!'' Rachel scoffed. ''A man like Garve Hutchins doesn't know the meaning of the word.

"We graduated high school in June. By July, Jemma realized she *was* pregnant. That same month, Jason came to the valley. Jemma had told Garve about her condition, and they'd had a terrible fight over it. He didn't want to get married, and she was deathly afraid to tell her folks. That's when she and I came up with—" she looked away for a moment. "—I guess you could call it a plan."

The story stalled a bit while Rachel sighed poignantly. "Jason seemed like the perfect solution. He was obviously taken with Jemma, and he seemed to be well fixed. Jemma was desperate. She was sure her father would beat her to death if he found out she was in the family way, and that damned Garve wouldn't do a thing. We were *both* desperate, me so worried about my best friend I was willing to do almost anything to help her, and Jemma nearly crazy with fear.

"It almost worked," Rachel said with a sad laugh. "Jason was so smitten he was easily maneuvered, and Jemma was positive he was on the verge of proposing. Only Garve reared his ugly head again.

"We were all at a dance, and in walked Garve. I saw Jemma notice him and start acting crazy, and I went over and pulled her aside. I said, 'Jemma, don't let that jerk ruin this for you. You're almost safe. Jason is in love with you, and don't let Garve ruin it.' Well, I guess she couldn't help herself, because the next thing I knew she and Jason had some kind of argument and out he goes. I could tell he was mad, and I started over to find out what had happened.

"But before I got to Jemma, Garve did. They

danced together, real chummy like, and I stewed on the sidelines, worrying that Jason would come back and see them. Lord, I was so scared for her. But Jemma told me later that Garve had said he'd changed his mind, that he would marry her. It was what she wanted to hear, and when Garve suggested it, she went out to his car with him.

"Jason came back. I saw him looking for Jemma, and he asked me where she was. I lied and told him I didn't know, so he asked someone else. He found her—out in Garve's car."

Rachel paused, her troubled air betraying her memories of the scene that had ensued. "If Garve hadn't shown up at that dance, Jemma and Jason would have gotten married. As it turned out, Garve skipped. Three weeks after Jason left, so did Garve. His whole family, too. As far as I know, none of them ever came back."

Tracy interjected, "But Jemma knew how to get in touch with Jason."

"Yes. She had his address, and when Garve left she wrote to Jason. She explained how she'd just discovered she was expecting and the baby was his."

"I have the letter, that one and two others. They were with the journals."

Astonishment altered Rachel's features. "You mean he kept them? All those years?"

Tracy nodded. "He really loved her, Rachel. Those entries in his journal were heartfelt."

Rachel's voice was soft, her manner reflective. "And he knew all the time the baby couldn't have been his.'' She sighed. ''That was something Jemma and I never thought of. We assumed Jason had been merely hurt the night of the dance, when he found her in Garve's car.''

The story was almost complete. But it was momentarily interrupted by the arrival of their lunch. When the waitress left the table, Tracy returned to the old tale. ''I think I know what happened next. Jemma had been deserted by two men, and Jase was the more desirable to her parents. Am I right?''

''Very right. When she couldn't put off telling them any longer, she chose to name Jason as the father. At least he was a decent man. Everyone in the valley thought the whole Hutchins clan a trashy bunch, as I already told you, but Jason had impressed folks. Anyway, the lie began.

''The sad thing was, Tracy, as the years passed, I think poor Jemma began to believe it. She actually believed Jason was living somewhere, suffering with love for her.''

''I think he was.'' Tracy sighed. ''I think he probably loved her every day of his life.''

Startled, Rachel exclaimed, ''How can you, of all people, say such a thing?''

''Oh, he loved me, too, but in a different way. I believe now that Jemma was Jase's first and most important love. It doesn't bother me, Rachel. Jase and I had four good years together. Actually, I feel very sad that he and Jemma's relationship ended so tragically.''

Rachel's eyes narrowed. ''Why did he give her the

ranch, Tracy? Jemma and I were sure it was because he really did think the baby was his, but that he couldn't face marriage any more than Garve could. Knowing the child wasn't his, why did he buy the ranch and give it to Jemma?''

"Read the journal, Rachel. He loved her. He was worried about her future. True, he couldn't get past what he considered her infidelity. But that didn't stop his feelings for Jemma.

"I also think the reason he kept half of it was so he could keep track of her. Through the financial reports, he knew Jemma was cared for.''

Rachel sat back, obviously deeply moved. "Oh, my. The tangled webs people weave.'' She straightened abruptly. "Well, I'm not proud of my part in it, but that's the story.''

Tracy was going over the information. "You said none of the Hutchins ever returned to the valley. Have you ever heard anything about them?''

"Garve, you mean? He's dead, Tracy. That news spread around even before Jemma died. It was odd how she took it, as though she had barely known him.''

"Was she terribly unhappy all her life?''

"Unhappy?'' Rachel frowned. "I really don't think so. The lie became so real to her, she developed a rather mournful miserable air. In a way, I think Jemma enjoyed her role as the mistreated woman. Poor Slade is the one who bore the brunt of the whole thing. Jemma's biggest fault was keeping the lie alive. It kept Slade on edge.''

Across the table, Tracy met Rachel's eyes sadly. "And you dedicated your life to the Dawsons. Why, Rachel?"

The woman shrugged. "I've asked myself that a thousand times, Tracy. I know at first it was because of Jemma. But after Slade came along, well, I loved him. He's as much my son as Jemma's. All I ever wanted was to see him finally happy." She gave Tracy a penetrating look. "Are *you* going to make him happy?"

Tracy swallowed. "He's got to know the truth, Rachel."

"Are you sure that's best?"

"He and I don't have a chance without it. What do you think?"

Rachel hesitated, then nodded reluctantly. "I only hope he doesn't turn against me," she said forlornly.

Tracy sighed. She was worried about that possibility, too.

Eleven

Tracy wanted to spend a little more time with Rachel Munley, so she decided to return to the ranch. With Slade away, the decision to tell him everything could remain open a little longer. The more she and Rachel discussed the past, however, the more necessary seeing Slade became.

True, there was a chance he would be so wounded by Rachel's part in the thirty-three-year-old duplicity that he would "turn against her," as Rachel had fearfully put it. There was also the chance that Tracy could present the facts in such a way that Slade would only be relieved. After all, what Rachel had done had been motivated by love for Jemma, certainly not by any desire for personal gain. And he must understand how much Rachel doted on him. He couldn't possibly sweep her years of devotion under the rug, no matter how deeply Rachel had been enmeshed in follies of the past.

Tracy mulled the situation over for the balance of the day. That night, at the dinner table, with Ben present, she asked, "Is Slade at Big Bluff alone?"

Ben replied first. "Sure is. He always stays after the horde leaves to put the cabin back in shape." He grinned. "His hunting buddies have a ball up there every year, but they're not much for cleaning up."

"Why?" Rachel asked. The question was directed at Tracy.

"I'm thinking of having Ben take me up there," Tracy replied, meeting Rachel's frown. "It's best to see him alone, Rachel."

"Yes, but..." Rachel drew a plainly frightened breath. "You've made your decision, then?"

"Not exactly. I want to see him. That's my only decision at this point."

Ben looked from one woman to the other. "What's going on?"

They hadn't yet told Ben that Tracy knew the truth, and Rachel proceeded to do so. Ben looked uncomfortable, and slightly guilty, as the story unfolded. When Rachel was finished, he gave Tracy a weak smile. "Sure hope you don't hold any of it against us, Tracy."

"I don't. I understand your loyalties—Rachel's to Slade, yours to Rachel. Would you be willing to escort me to Big Bluff in the morning?"

Ben nodded thoughtfully. "It's not an easy trip in this weather."

The baby came to mind, along with the list of dos and don'ts Dr. Lessing had given her. There had been no reason to cover a horseback ride, so it hadn't been mentioned. Would it be risky?

Tracy frowned. "Dolly has a very easy gait. How does she perform in snow?"

"Oh, no problem with Dolly. She's as surefooted as they come. But it's cold out, Tracy."

"How far is it, Ben? How long would it take?"

"A couple of hours at least. Are you sure you want to do it?"

"I'm sure I want to see Slade," she answered, silently going over the problem. She'd been feeling much better, and Dr. Lessing had assured her she was really in excellent health. He had also told her not to curtail her activities, that there was no reason to avoid anything she would normally do.

But a two-hour horseback ride?

"Could we rest periodically?" she asked.

"Rest?"

"I mean, get out of the saddle and walk around a bit, just to change positions."

"Well, sure." Ben's puzzlement was reflected in Rachel's eyes, and brother and sister regarded Tracy with unspoken questions.

Tracy dispelled their curiosity with a warm smile, not ready to confide in anyone yet. "I'd like to go. I wanted to see Big Bluff last summer, and it must be beautiful with snow."

"It's a beautiful spot, all right," Ben agreed. "We'll leave about nine in the morning, give the sun a chance to warm things up, okay?"

"And you'll have to dress real warm," Rachel warned.

"I will. I have a ski suit with me. It keeps out the cold, believe me."

The next morning they started for the mountains. Rachel had wound two scarves around Tracy's lower face and neck, and with the hood of her ski parka up, nothing showed but her eyes. The air was crisp, but the sun was bright, and riding Dolly through the snow was a delight.

They stopped every half hour and got down, walking around for a few minutes in the winter wonderland, then remounted and continued the journey. Dolly followed Ben's horse with very little guidance, and Tracy's mind was free to wander.

She had the journal with her and felt a certain amount of nervousness about suddenly popping in on Slade. He was bound to be surprised.

It was a play-it-by-ear situation, Tracy admitted. She had no clear idea of how the meeting might go, although visualizing how she would like it to go was easy. All she could be sure of was how she'd present her side of the story. Slade's input was completely unpredictable. It was impossible to foresee what he might do.

Telling Slade all she knew was going to be very difficult. How should she really handle it? She couldn't just hit the subject without some preliminary conversation. In fact, she still wasn't completely sure she should tell him at all. If he didn't really love her, what was the point? Maybe she should start with what he felt for her. Everything hinged on that in the long run.

As they left the valley floor and followed the ascending trail into the mountains, the snow grew deeper, the cold a bit sharper. She felt fine, Tracy realized gratefully, mentally checking her physical reactions to Dolly's careful steps. The little mare was as cautious as if she knew she carried a precious burden, and the thought made Tracy smile behind the warmth of the scarves.

Tracy felt that the wonder of the baby created a glow in her heart that could never be snuffed out. And she wanted to share it with Slade so much. She wanted to give him this, she realized, this priceless gift.

The first hint that they were approaching the cabin came in the form of woodsmoke hovering at the tops of the tall pine trees. Tracy's heart skipped a beat. "Are we almost there?" she called.

"Almost," Ben replied over his shoulder. "Are you all right?"

"Never been better. This was an incredible ride, Ben. I loved it."

Whenever Tracy thought of Slade, the image was influenced by his sensuality. It was something she couldn't prevent. His intense lovemaking was so much a part of him, she couldn't separate it from his other qualities. Now, as they approached the log cabin, a pretty little building with two front windows spaced precisely on either side of an oak door, that was what was uppermost in Tracy's thoughts. Oddly, instead of thinking of all they had to speak of, her mind rushed ahead to what might be once they had things settled.

Yes, she had no doubt that she was in love with Slade Dawson. She loved him, and his incredible body, and his tender lovemaking—and she wished all their problems were already behind them and that she was coming to the cabin for a night of nothing but love. To be alone with him in this wintry paradise, to melt into his arms...to whisper her love...

Tracy jolted herself out of her reverie. This dream was beautiful, but not very realistic, not with what was really ahead of her.

The cabin door opened as they reined the horses to a halt. Slade stepped outside, and Tracy could see he didn't recognize her. "Ben? What are you doing up here?" he called, walking over to them with a perplexed expression.

He looked so tall and straight and handsome that Tracy's heart did a flip. She pulled the scarves down below her chin so he could see her face. "He brought me, Slade."

"Tracy?" Utter amazement registered on his face, and he veered in her direction. "Here, let me help you down." His hands went around her waist, which was bulky from her layers of clothing, not from her condition. No one would be able to detect her pregnancy from her figure, she knew, no one except Slade.

"What are you doing here?" Slade asked, studying her intently.

Tracy smiled. "You're not upset I came, are you?"

"I'm baffled." Slade turned to Ben. "Aren't you getting down, Ben?"

"Naw. I'm gonna head right back, Slade. You two have fun," he threw out lightly, and turned his mount's head.

"Go on into the cabin," Slade commanded Tracy. "I'll see to Dolly and be right in."

Tracy hesitated a moment, watching him lead the gray mare away. So far, so good. They'd gotten over the initial meeting with only a normal amount of surprise. She hurried into the cabin, delighted with its warm, homey atmosphere. A blazing fire in a very large fireplace dominated the main room, and while she worked at shedding her heavy clothing she took a peek into a small but adequate kitchen, two bedrooms and a tiny bathroom.

The place was totally masculine. There wasn't a frippery or a ruffle anywhere in sight. It had no apparent color scheme, yet it was warm and comfortable. Stripped down to just her jeans and white turtleneck sweater, Tracy sat on the hearth and absorbed the wonderful heat while she finger-combed her hair, trying to bring some shape back to her hat-flattened hairstyle.

The door opened, and Slade came in. He set the canvas bag Rachel had provided for a few clothes on the floor and walked over to the fire. "I'm awfully curious, Tracy," he said, giving her a thorough once-over.

"I'm sure you are." She smiled tentatively. "I wanted to see you."

"Obviously. The burning question is, why? After my less-than-successful visit to San Francisco I thought I'd never see you again." She looked better than she had in California he realized. Of course, her cheeks were pink from the cold, so maybe that was a premature observation. But her eyes were brighter. Lord, she was beautiful. That white sweater had a stylish looseness, yet there was no hiding the most arousing body he'd ever seen and enjoyed.

He tore his gaze away from her and took the nearest chair, a royal-blue burlap-covered chair that was his favorite. Many, many times he'd sat right here and stared into the fire, thinking of Tracy. Now here she was. Even with her perched on the hearth with her hands extended to the dancing flames, it didn't seem quite real.

"I thought that, too," she admitted, giving him a sidelong glance. "But things have changed."

"What things?" The question wasn't stated kindly. The last time they'd spoken of change it had been to agree that nothing of importance *could* change.

Tracy avoided answering immediately by asking, "Could I have something hot to drink?"

"Good God, yes!" Slade jumped up. "What would you like? I know, some coffee and brandy. That will warm you up fast."

"No brandy. And I'd rather have herbal tea, if you have it."

"Tea? Brandy would be better, Tracy. It takes the chill off right now."

She shook her head. "Thank you, no. Just some tea."

Slade started for the kitchen. "Are you hungry?"

Rising, Tracy followed him. "I could eat something."

He began pulling things from the refrigerator, some cold meat and condiments. "May I help?" Tracy asked.

"If you want to. There's bread in that box on the counter." Slade filled the kettle and set it on the stove.

"The cabin is nice, Slade. I like it," Tracy commented as she began putting a sandwich together. "Would you like one?"

"I already ate, thanks."

How civilized they were being, Tracy thought. That was a good sign, yet she knew how quickly passion could flare between them, and not only sexual passion. Slade could switch moods at the drop of a hat. Right now he was puzzled, but not so impatient to learn the reason for this unexpected visit that he couldn't give her time to eat. But Tracy sensed that once food was out of the way she could expect some pressure.

When they were back in the central room, seated before the fire again, she chewed very slowly, alternating small bites of the tasty sandwich with sips of invigorating hot tea.

"Did you get an elk?" she asked.

"You're eating it," Slade said with a wicked grin.

"I am?" Frowning, she opened the bread and looked at the meat. It looked like roast beef, and finally she shrugged. "Well, it's delicious," she declared, taking another bite.

Slade laughed heartily, and Tracy smiled sheepishly. "Did I do something funny?"

"You're a sweetheart," he returned. "You almost couldn't eat it, could you?"

She colored prettily at the endearment. "Pretty silly, huh?"

He shook his head. "Not silly, not at all. Everybody's got their own feelings about wild meat, Tracy. Some people would rather eat elk or deer or bear than anything else. Then there are those who'd rather starve than dare anything beyond beef or pork."

She made a face. "Bear?"

"It's good. You might like it, too."

"I might...but I doubt it."

He laughed again, and Tracy marveled at the deep, rumbling sound. Had she ever heard him really laugh before, without cynicism?

She looked at Slade perceptively. It was impossible to look at him and not be aware of his maleness. It was what she had first seen in Slade, and it was just as impressive today. He was wearing a blue plaid woolen shirt with the cuffs turned back, and she could see the white knit of long-sleeved underwear where the cuffs stopped. Also, from the fit of his jeans, she suspected he was wearing long johns. It was only sensible in this weather, but it added to his rugged appearance.

He was the father of the child she carried. This big, handsome man had made love to her, and that love had created the small life within her body. Suddenly very moved, Tracy had to look away from him, afraid she might blurt her condition out. It was too soon. They had a lot to get through first.

Tracy stood up, carried her empty plate to the kitchen and made another cup of tea. "I've been packing everything in my house, Slade." She returned to her chair.

Slade sat up straighter. "Are you moving?"

"Yes. I've been planning to leave San Francisco for some time now."

"To go where?"

"I'm not sure." She drew a deep breath. "To be perfectly honest, I keep thinking about…Montana."

"Tracy…" Instantly Slade was out of his chair and kneeling beside her. He clasped her hands in his, and the expression on his face made her heart pound. "Are you ready to listen to me now?" he asked hoarsely. "Will you let me tell you how I feel about you?"

She nodded. "That's one of the reasons I'm here," she said softly.

Slade released her hands and dropped his head into her lap, burrowing his hands behind her in a massive embrace. "What changed your mind? Oh, sweetheart, I didn't have a drop of hope."

He raised his head to look at her. "You already know it, don't you. You know I'm in love with you."

"I...I couldn't let myself know it," she whispered, touching his face with warm fingertips. "You really do love me?"

"I love you," he replied simply. Then he smiled. "It's your turn."

Tracy swallowed and looked away. "I have a lot to tell you."

"There's only one thing I want to hear right now. Say it, Tracy." Slade took her chin and turned her face back to him. "Do you love me, too?"

How could she not answer such a plea? "I... Yes. I love you, too."

She was swept into an immediate, heated embrace and felt Slade take possession of her lips. His mouth was hungry on hers. She felt his hands lift her sweater and roam her bare skin, lighting fires wherever they lingered.

This wasn't what she'd planned. They had to talk. If everything went well, they could make love for days. She tore her mouth from his. "Slade, please," she gasped. "There are things—"

"There's nothing more important," he growled, standing and drawing her up with him. He swung her up into his arms. "I need you so badly, I'm on fire," he said thickly, starting for one of the bedrooms.

Her heart was pounding. This was how she wanted him, strong, masterful, hot. But the time wasn't right.

"Slade, it's about Jase and your mother. We have to talk," she whispered in his ear as they cleared the bedroom door.

She felt him stiffen, and he allowed her feet to slide to the floor. Sexual passion hadn't disappeared from his expression, but another facet had been added, giving him an ominous look. "What about them?" he demanded gruffly.

"I found an old journal. It's one of Jase's personal diaries. I brought it along."

There was so very much in the look they exchanged: anger, resentment, pain, love. Finally Slade passed a hand over his face in a weary gesture. "Do you think I give a damn about anything he might have written?"

"Slade!" It hadn't occurred to Tracy that he might simply refuse to give the journal any credence. Rachel had seen its authenticity immediately. "I showed it to Rachel, and she admitted it was true," she said in a hopeful voice. "Slade, you've got to at least give it a chance."

"The man doesn't deserve a chance!"

"No, but we do!"

Slade looked at her soberly. "What are you getting at?"

She swallowed nervously. "After Rachel read the journal she told me what really happened thirty-three years ago. It's not what you were raised to believe."

His eyes were growing stormy, his face losing every trace of warmth. Without warning he whirled and walked from the room, and when Tracy meekly trailed after him she found him stirring the fire with vicious jabs of a long poker.

She didn't speak, merely curled up in a chair and waited. He had to absorb what she'd told him, even though she had barely scratched the surface. Just the mention of Jase's name had put him on the defensive. Tracy could see that her suggestion that events hadn't been what he'd been told all his life was causing an emotional battle within him. She watched the muscles of his back and shoulders work as he rearranged the wood on the grate with the poker. He finally added a chunk of wood. Then he stood up. "Where is it?"

"The journal? I'll get it." Quickly Tracy went to her canvas bag and pulled the book out. She carried it over to him. "I've marked some pages with paper clips," she said gently, offering the faded book.

Slade stared at it for an inordinately long time, as though it were something harmful. "Take it, Slade. Please. You've got to know the truth. It's the only way you and I..." She let the sentence dangle, knowing he understood exactly what she was implying.

His chest expanded with a deeply drawn breath, and at long last he accepted the journal. While he settled into the blue chair again, Tracy took her cup into the kitchen. She reheated the water in the kettle and prepared a fresh cup of tea, finally returning to the living room. Slade was staring into the fire, the book closed on his lap.

"Did you read it?"

"I read it. What did Rachel tell you?"

His words were so cold that Tracy felt as if she

were dying inside. She tried to remember that only minutes ago they had told each other of their love, and at the same time she worried that Slade was going to do exactly as she had feared, transfer the hatred he'd harbored for Jase to Rachel and maybe his mother. Shivering even though the room was very comfortable, she sat down.

She couldn't stop now. When she spoke, it was with a remarkable calmness, considering her quaking interior. "Before I tell you the entire story, I want to ask you something. Do you know how much Rachel loves you?"

"What?" Slade's frown only enhanced his glower. "What the hell has that—"

She didn't let him finish. "She loved your mother the same way, Slade. Rachel Munley has devoted her life to the Dawsons, first your mother, then you. I guess what I'm really asking is, do you appreciate it? Do you love her in return?"

"Tracy, for crying out loud!"

"Does it embarrass you to talk about it? Slade, I know flowery words and sentiment don't come easily for you, but I couldn't possibly live my life with a man who keeps every feeling good and bad, bottled up inside himself."

"Is that fair? Didn't I just tell you how I feel about you? Didn't I say it 'flowery' enough?"

"You said it beautifully. And I believe you. If I didn't, I wouldn't have told you about the journal."

"Why not? Isn't it the real reason you came?" Slade tossed the journal onto the seat of the chair and walked over to the window. With his hands thrust into the side pockets of his jeans, he glared at the wintry scene outside the cabin.

Tracy sighed. She put the cup down, walked over to him and put her arms around him. She felt his sudden intake of breath, but she maintained her position and laid her cheek right between his shoulder blades. "I came to see *you*," she said huskily. "Don't mistrust every move people make, darling."

He turned in her arms, and brought her head to his chest. "No one's ever called me darling before," he whispered. "Tracy, I love you. I think I fell for you the minute you got off that damned helicopter."

"It's possible," she murmured with a smile.

"But that doesn't mean I believe that journal."

She stiffened.

"It's nothing but a pack of lies, written by a man trying to expiate a guilty conscience," Slade continued harshly.

Placing her palms against his chest, Tracy pushed herself from his arms. "I'm sorry you see it that way."

"Are you going to tell me what Rachel said?"

Tracy regarded him with a cool, steady look. "No, I'm not. You're not ready to hear it."

"I'll ask her myself," Slade returned darkly.

"Go right ahead. I doubt she'll tell you a thing," she retorted.

A sudden weariness overtook her. This hadn't gone the way she had hoped, and the strenuous ride was catching up with her. "I'd like to lie down for a while. Would you mind?"

"Are you feeling all right?" Slade said with concern.

"Just tired. A short rest is all I need."

"You can use that bedroom," he said, directing her to the room opposite the one he had carried her into.

"Thank you." After getting the canvas bag, Tracy walked to the bedroom. "I wish you'd think about the things we talked about," she said softly before entering the room.

He didn't answer, and with a sigh Tracy went inside and closed the door. She slipped off her boots and crawled beneath the blankets, snuggling down with a yawn and a prayer. Maybe Slade needed a little time, and right now she desperately needed a nap.

"Tracy, are you all right?"

The room was dark, but the door was open and light outlined Slade's tall, slender build. His face was shadowed, though, and Tracy squinted at him. "What time is it?"

"Nearly six. I was getting worried about you."

Tracy sat up in bed. "I slept all afternoon. I'm sorry, Slade."

"Hey, you were tired, you slept—if that's all there is to it. Have you been ill?" Slade recalled too well how peaked she had looked in San Francisco.

"No, I haven't been ill." Tracy swung her feet to the floor. "What smells so good?" she asked, sniffing the air appreciatively.

"Dinner. It's almost ready."

"Great. Let me freshen up a bit and I'll join you."

Tracy couldn't help smiling over the thought of Slade doing kitchen duty. When she entered the delicious-smelling room ten minutes later, she saw at once that he knew his way around quite well. The meal he was preparing wasn't fancy, by any means, but the meat browning in the iron skillet and the vegetables steaming away looked very appetizing.

Tracy took her cue from Slade's cordial but impersonal "Everything's ready. I just have to dish up."

To Tracy, sitting down to the first meal they had ever shared was meaningful. She wondered if Slade was aware that they'd never eaten together.

It wasn't until Slade got up and brought a mug of coffee for himself and a cup of tea for Tracy that the previous subject came up. "I read the journal again," Slade offered, adding a splash of milk to his coffee.

Tracy's spirit ignited. "You did?"

Slade stirred the mixture in his mug with more attention than it merited. "I'll give him this much—I think he believed what he wrote."

"But you don't believe it."

"How can I? A woman must know when a man— what I mean is, doesn't a woman know?" Slade raked his hair, agitated. "Oh, hell, you know what I mean. Maybe Jase never had his condition checked by a doctor. Or maybe the doctor was wrong."

Tracy nodded. "And you feel a woman must know who the father of her child is."

"Yes." Slade eyed her intently. "She does, doesn't she?"

"I'm sure she does," Tracy answered softly.

"In that case, how can I believe anyone but my mother?"

Tracy's heart ached for Slade, and she looked away. She had to open his mind up, to create a chink in his self-protective armor. It was easy to see how he must feel about suddenly reading that the man he had always been told was his father had actually been sterile. Yes, she could go into Rachel's more detailed narrative, but would that work? Perhaps it was time to tell him what had caused her original doubt—her own pregnancy. Every nerve in her body jumped to full alert at the thought. Once he knew, there was no turning back. When he learned of the baby, their futures were forever intertwined. She wanted to be sure she was doing the right thing before telling him.

He looked unhappy, desperate, as though pleading for acceptance of his position in the matter, the one thing she couldn't give him. He *had* to face the truth, however painful. He was not Jason Moorland's son, and if Slade didn't come to grips with that, then for Tracy there was no future for them.

The time for tripping around the truth was past. Tracy took a deep breath. "Slade, I'm going to tell you what Rachel told me. I know it's going to hurt, but I want you to listen to the whole story before you fly off the handle. Will you try to do that?"

There was a long pause before he agreed, but finally Tracy began.

Twelve

Slade didn't take her news the way Tracy had expected. With every new twist in the tale he grew more withdrawn. At one point he got up to refill their mugs, and he also brought the brandy bottle to the table and liberally laced his coffee with it.

She refused a similar dose but couldn't fault Slade for needing something stronger than caffeine. In his position she might look for a crutch, too, she acknowledged, wondering just how she might react if suddenly blasted with such a shocking revelation. It made her speak very gently and express compassion for Jemma's youthful indiscretions and Rachel's obsessive loyalty.

"Now you can see why I asked you about your feelings for Rachel, Slade. I've been deeply concerned about how this might affect your relationship.'' Tracy felt his remoteness and shrank inwardly, fearing the worst. Even so, she was unprepared for his response.

''Is that all?'' he asked brusquely.

Her eyes reflected her dismay. ''That's all you have to say?''

Slade got to his feet. ''I need to think about this.'' Plates clattered as he stacked them. Tracy rose and began gathering up the used utensils. ''I'd rather you didn't help,'' he said sharply.

Stunned, she dropped the handful of knives and forks on the table and stepped back. ''Whatever you say.'' Blinded by sudden, searing tears, she hurried into the living room, telling herself that it was natural for him to want to be alone.

The fire had died down, and blinking at the tears, Tracy added several chunks of wood to the glowing embers, watching them catch and blaze. She sank to the hearth and stared morosely at the flickering flames. A sudden gust of wind hit the cabin, sounding mournful in the silent night, and a deep sense of the cabin's isolation made her shiver. Slade's movements in the kitchen were easy to follow—water running, the clank of dishes and metalware, steps taken between sink and table.

What was he thinking? Was he seeing memories of Jemma and Rachel reinforcing the lie? No doubt he was. He had to be wondering about Garve Hutchins, too, and suffering over this new image of Jason Moorland. Putting Jase into so different a role from the one

Slade had lived with all of his life had to be difficult for him.

Tracy sighed sadly. What would she do if Slade couldn't deal with it? There was too much at stake to just give up. She could raise the baby alone. It was done every day. But she wanted this child to have both a father and a mother.

Slade's retreating into that shell was really the only thing standing in the way. He was conveying the same "hands off" attitude she had endured last summer, which was a big hurdle to clear.

When Slade finally joined her, he went immediately to the fire. He poked it a few times with the poker and added another block of wood, even though it was blazing nicely. Tracy moved from the hearth and settled uneasily into a chair. She was aware of his every movement, and she was sure he had to be the same with her. They were so alone out here. There was nothing to focus on but each other. But neither of them was comfortable, and the air was vibrant with disquietude.

Involuntarily Tracy's fingers locked over her lower abdomen in a protective gesture. The past didn't matter now. It was the future that was important. She had to get Slade to communicate somehow. By shutting her out, he was unwittingly cutting himself off from his child.

"The wind is coming up," she commented casually.

Slade turned his back to the fire and faced her with his feet firmly planted, his arms folded, in an almost belligerent stance. "A storm's moving in," he stated coolly.

She was determined to incite conversation, and she ignored his standoffish attitude. "When I was ten, my father took me to Tahoe for a weekend of skiing. He rented a cabin in the mountains—one quite similar to this, actually. We arrived there on a Friday evening with plans to ski the entire weekend." Tracy smiled invitingly, doing a very good job of pretending there wasn't a bit of discord between them. "Only during Friday night a blizzard hit. By morning we were so snowed in there wasn't a chance of getting to the slopes. The storm raged for two days, and we spent the weekend by the fire, playing checkers and eating popcorn. As it turned out, it was one of the nicest weekends of my childhood."

"Is your father still living?"

Tracy heard a dark note of envy in Slade's question. "Yes, I'm happy to say he lives in San Francisco. But my mother died when I was very young. I have no clear memories of her."

The envy disappeared from his voice. "So you were raised with a father and no mother, just the opposite of me."

Her heart turned over with hope. At least they were talking, and although Slade sounded bewildered and a bit reserved, he was not angry. "Ideally children need both parents, but Dad did a good job," she said softly. "You were close to your mother, weren't you?"

Slade sat down, stretched out his long legs and

stared broodingly into the fire. "I didn't really know her, did I? I thought I did, but it was all a lie."

"Of course it wasn't all a lie, Slade. Don't think that. Her feelings for you were real. They had nothing to do with—"

He gave her a hard look. "Don't presume too much, Tracy. All you know is what you read in that journal and heard from Rachel. You're in no position to judge anything beyond that."

"Well, no, I agree, but—"

Slade looked back at the fire. "We weren't very close. I think we both tried, but we never quite made the grade," he said quietly.

Tracy felt her heart breaking. "Oh, Slade, I'm so sorry," she whispered.

He didn't want her pity, and he stated gruffly, "It's no big deal, Tracy."

Tracy was aghast. No big deal? A boy raised with a lie about his father and a mother he hadn't felt close to? It was quite a big deal. No wonder he was so cautious with his feelings. No wonder he had turned all his passion and affection toward the ranch. The Double J had represented solidity, safety.

But Rachel had been there, too, and she must have played a very big part in his life. "Were you close to Rachel?" Tracy asked quietly, daring to broach the subject again.

It was a moment before Slade replied, with a non-committal "I guess so."

Tracy sighed, seeing another wall between Slade and his feelings. She was startled when he turned to her abruptly and asked, "What about us? You're obviously satisfied that I'm not Jason Moorland's son. Is that enough?"

"Enough for what, Slade?"

He drew a deep breath. "Will you marry me?"

Surely this wasn't his idea of a moving marriage proposal? He had posed the question as though he'd asked her the time of day. They were sitting at least five feet apart, with all sorts of ambiguities in the air. In fact, he looked as though he expected a flat turndown. Was that all he expected from life, more heartache?

"I don't think we're ready to talk about marriage."

"Speak for yourself. I'm ready. I want you, Tracy."

"You want me in your bed, Slade. That takes care of the nights nicely, but what about the days?"

His frown showed genuine perplexity. "What do you mean?"

She hesitated, wanting to say this right. "Do you realize that tonight was the first time we sat down to dinner together? Are you aware of how little we've really talked? I don't have the foggiest idea of your personal tastes."

He was watching her with an odd light in his eyes. "Is that really important?"

"Aren't you even a little curious about *me*?" She smiled faintly, with just a hint of amusement. "You wouldn't even know what to give me for a Christmas present. You don't know any more about me than I know about you."

"I know I love you," he said grimly. "That's enough for me. And I won't apologize for wanting you in my bed."

"Slade, don't you understand at all what I'm getting at?" Tracy sighed.

"I know you better than you think I do. I know you're beautiful and exciting. I know you're intelligent and nosy as hell. You've got courage. I don't care what your favorite color is, I know what I like, and I like you in blue. And I know what I'd give you for Christmas, too, another one of those sexy nightgowns you wear, a blue one, with skinny straps and a long skirt. Just like you were wearing that night on the balcony."

Tracy froze when Slade got up and came over to her. He knelt in front of her, the hard muscles of his stomach pressing into her knees. He grasped the arms of her chair, effectively surrounding her. His gaze bored into her. "The heart of the matter isn't what I like to read, Tracy, it's do you love me enough to accept me as I am?"

Stung, Tracy stared into the depths of his eyes. She should never underestimate Slade, she realized. While he wasn't much of a talker, he was definitely a thinker. And what result had she come to Montana for, ridden a horse two hours for? Wasn't it this, Slade looking at her with love?

"I love you," she whispered. "I love you more than I've ever loved anyone."

"Is that really true?"

She saw hope ignite in his eyes, and he moved his

hands to her waist. "It's true," she said huskily. His head came to her breasts, and she wrapped her arms around it, cradling it tenderly.

"Don't pick it apart, Tracy. We'll have years to learn about each other. Marry me, sweetheart. I swear I'll do everything I can to make you happy."

"You must share yourself, Slade," she whispered brokenly. He had touched her deeply, and it showed in her voice. "That's all I ask. I need to feel a part of you."

His head came up, and his rugged features betrayed his inner torment. "You are a part of me. The best part." His mouth neared hers. "Let me kiss you, let me love you," he whispered. "I need you."

Her resolve to maintain a reasonable distance dissolved as his lips brushed hers. It wasn't within her power to deny what Slade made her feel, and it never had been, not even at the start. Now, true, they were on the brink of a serious commitment, and it was complicated by some still-very-provoking unknowns. But recognizing that did nothing to quiet the rushed beat of her heart or the sudden, piercing desire he elicited.

His lips traveled to her throat. "You smell like no other woman alive," he whispered, feathering small kisses along the line of the high-necked sweater, his breath heating her skin. At her waist his fingers slowly worked the bottom of the sweater upward, bunching it until he touched warm flesh. Then, beneath the white knit, his hands went around her, drawing her forward.

Her thighs relaxed, allowing him to move between them. She and Slade held each other with sudden, overpowering need. He dropped kisses on her forehead, her cheeks, her chin, and finally his lips covered hers. Tracy was weakened by the emotion that shot through her. She felt inundated not only by immediate and intense physical response but by a response of the heart, as well. What was logic in the face of so much love?

Her mouth opened wider as Slade's tongue danced beguilingly. This was leading straight to the bedroom, and Tracy didn't care. She loved this man, and at the moment the knowledge that he was withholding a part of himself from her, right along with the rest of the world, really wasn't very important. His aura, his hands, his lips, were all that had meaning.

She let him urge her out of the chair and down to the floor, onto the thick rug in front of the fireplace. The flames in the fireplace were leaping wildly, but they were a mere spark compared to the flames licking at her insides. Momentarily startled, she watch Slade rise and extinguish the lamps, returning to the rug with only the orange-and-red flickering of the fire lighting the room.

The cold wind buffeting the cabin's exterior seemed far away. Slade, lying beside her, stretched them both out to a full-length embrace. Tracy's sigh was ragged, a sound of needful acquiescence as she lifted her arms to his neck and clung to him. His body moved subtly against hers, every steely inch seeking a closer union.

Kisses melted into another and another. The quivering need became more demanding. His hands moved from her breasts to lay claim to every part of her, searing her through jeans and sweater and undergarments.

But through the cloud of passion, Tracy felt panic developing. It was suddenly crucial that she tell him about the baby before they made love. He had a right to know. He deserved the same chance at the kind of happiness a child brought as she did. Yes, there might be problems, but the love they shared would smooth the way. She could no longer deny him this precious gift.

She was frightened but driven. Her hands went to his cheeks, urging his head up. "Slade, I have something to tell you," she whispered.

Slade's groan was pure misery. "No more, Tracy. I've heard enough for today."

"I think you'll like this," she said, her tone entreating.

His gaze moved over her face. Damn, he thought, she was beautiful, and he didn't want any more talk. What he wanted was to undress her and make love to her, first here, then move to the bed, *his* bed. He had so much desire inside him that he was ready to explode, and he visualized a long night of love.

Besides, he was almost afraid to hear it; he had enough to deal with now. But he could see in her eyes that she was determined. With an "All right, let's get it over with" look, he finally nodded, displaying a little of the impatience he was feeling.

She stole a breath. "Slade, you're going to be a father in May." Her words didn't sink in immediately. At first he looked at her as though she were speaking Greek. His first clear thought was that he had misunderstood. "What did you say?" he asked, a puzzled look in his eyes.

It was out, and already she felt better. "You're going to be a father in May," she repeated softly, and before she had finished speaking Slade had buried his face in the curve of her throat. His heart was pounding so furiously that he could hear it, and waves of shock and disbelief assailed him.

Tracy stroked the back of his neck tenderly. "You do understand, don't you?" she whispered.

He raised his head slowly. "Are you sure?"

"Very."

That was why she had looked pale and unwell in San Francisco. Had she known then? That was why the ride up had worn her out! No wonder she had slept all afternoon.

He kept staring at her now, understanding all the little changes he'd noticed. He wet his lips with an odd nervousness. "You shouldn't have made the trip up here. Are you sure you're all right?"

Her laughter rippled. "I'm fine. I had some unpleasantness with nausea for a while, but it's passed." Her fingers went to his lips and traced their outline. "Are you happy about it?"

Happy? Could one word describe what he was feeling? A baby...his very own son or daughter, to love and care for? Happy wasn't sufficient. He was elated, filled with a joy he'd never before experienced.

And, good Lord, he had Tracy on the floor! She might catch a chill—or worse.

Hastily Slade scrambled to his feet. "Come on, this isn't the place for a mother-to-be."

She laughed again. "Slade, I'm fine. Don't worry," she exclaimed, though she let herself be pulled upright. "You didn't answer my question. Are you happy about the baby?"

His emotions choked him, and his thoughts tripped over each other. He wanted to shout, to do something dumb, like dancing a wild jig. But all he did was gather her close and whisper, "I'm happy, I'm very happy."

Her sigh sounded contented, even to her own ears. Tracy snuggled closer, wrapping her arms around his waist. "I wanted to tell you all day, but—"

A painful realization dawned on him, and he pushed away from her just enough to see her face. "You almost didn't tell me. Why not, Tracy?"

Her green eyes were guileless. "I was afraid," she answered simply.

"Of me?" Something wrenched within him, a soul-aching vision of a future without Tracy. It was clear now why she'd tried to explain and clarify the past. As surely as a forest creature protecting its young, Tracy had been smoothing the jagged path, creating a safe haven for the baby's arrival. He hadn't given her much cooperation. Little wonder she had been reluctant to tell him.

Cursing under his breath, Slade nestled her head against his chest. Either she felt safer with him or she had decided to take the risk for some other reason.

He was happier and more miserable than anyone deserved to be, and all at the same time. Guilt warred with bliss, uncertainty with unspoken promises. The warm, soft woman in his arms stirred. ''Slade?''

''I love you,'' he whispered, all the joy and confusion of his emotional quandary in the three words.

''I love you, too. We have a ways to go, but we can work things out, darling,'' Tracy murmured, raising her chin to press her lips to his throat. Then, on tiptoe, she reached his mouth. ''Don't we have some unfinished business?'' she whispered.

His arms tightened in an instant response to the seductiveness of her question. Yes, they had unfinished business, and he wanted her so desperately he hurt. But...

''Is it all right?'' he asked fearfully. ''Can you...?''

Her laugh was pure magic, like the peal of bells on a clear day. ''Of course I can.''

He almost swept her up from the floor but stopped himself in time, afraid he might be too rough. With his arm around her waist, he led her to his bedroom. He switched on a lamp and turned down the bed, restraining the wild drumming of his blood. He was positive she was more fragile than before and vowed to be gentle.

Tracy watched him, and when the blankets and pillows were to his satisfaction, he turned to her. His hands were gentle on her face and his kiss was only a whisper of his previous passion. She sensed he was holding back, and sensed, too, the reason for it. She smiled knowingly. "I'm not made of glass, Slade."

"I don't want to hurt you." Almost cautiously, he lifted the sweater over her head.

She wanted him as he had been before, wild, hot, demanding, and she gave him an alluring look as she reached behind her, unsnapped her bra and let the straps slide down her arms. Unbound, her nipples leaped to rigidity, and she saw Slade draw in a tortured breath. She took his hands and brought them to her breasts. "Love me," she whispered sensuously. "Do what you want to, darling. I need you as badly as you need me."

"Tracy—" It was a hot gasp, a mating cry, and he tumbled them both to the bed, his mouth hungry as he took one lush nipple, enclosing the other in an avid grasp.

"Yes," she whispered raggedly. "Yes. That's what I want." Her hands shook as they worked at the buttons on his shirt only to find a layer of thermal underwear instead of the hot skin she sought. "Take it off," she insisted.

Slade pulled his shirt away. Then his hands moved to his belt buckle, opened it and unzipped his fly. Their hasty undressing took only seconds, but it seemed to last forever. Finally Slade was back with her, drawing the cotton flannel sheet and blankets over the two of them, enclosing her within the circle of his arms.

"You're so beautiful," he groaned hoarsely as his hands roamed beneath the blankets. "So perfect."

Tracy's eyes closed. She was enraptured by her own exploration. His body was hard, as were his chest, his belly, his long, hair-roughened legs. But especially that incredible maleness between his thighs, and boldly she lingered there, encircling, stroking.

Slade rose to his elbows, and his mouth possessed hers in a long, consuming kiss. "I love you more than life," he whispered, feasting his eyes on the beauty of her face. "Tracy, you will marry me, won't you?"

She sighed softly. "I want to."

"How can you have any doubt with the baby coming?"

She couldn't talk about it now, and she pulled his head down. "Kiss me," she whispered. "I've thought of this for so long."

Slade's lips met hers, skillful, teasing, touching her heart, her soul. The heat of his body was erotic under the covers, causing a blossoming intimacy far exceeding anything she had thought possible. Oh, yes, there was lust between her and Slade. She would never question it again. But that wasn't all there was between them. There were layers and layers to love, each one containing its own unique nuances and special feelings. At the core, if a man and woman didn't have lust, did they have love?

Slade wielded a tremendous sexual power over her, but that was the way she wanted it. The male, strong, dominant, the female, warming herself with his fire.

It was the tone of their relationship, and Tracy basked in its glow.

His hands slid over her, and her inner fires built to a blaze of desire. She could feel the trembling within him and the might in his body, and she knew she hadn't exaggerated an iota when she'd told Slade she had never loved anyone so much. His kisses weren't just exciting, they were addictive, drugging. She would never get enough of him, never.

Soon kisses weren't enough. Her body strained to capture his touch, writhing an invitation, a plea. She was burning for him, aching, and when his hand skimmed down her smooth stomach, it found her thighs parted and waiting.

He was gifted with a wonderful knowledge of feminine mysteries, she realized, for his touch was tender and expert. A pleasure as intense as an electrical shock arose from his sensual massage, and she knew just how needful she'd been when almost immediately wave after pulsating wave of incredible ecstasy erased the past, the present and even the future from her mind. She moaned, gripping him tightly, clinging to the rapture for a breathless eternity.

While her heart calmed, he held her, brushing her hair back, caressing her cheek, her shoulder, her arm. "You work a special kind of magic on me, Slade," she murmured with a shaky laugh.

He laughed softly. "With you and me, there is a special magic. There always was, right from day one."

"Yes," she said. "There always was."

He touched her mouth in an agonizingly tender kiss. "I love you," he whispered.

"I love you, too." She urged him on top of her, opening her legs, and when he was settled, she pressed against his masculinity. "Make love to me," she whispered.

His breath was ragged. "I want it perfect for you."

"It is, it couldn't be more perfect. Don't wait any longer, darling. I know you must be hurting."

With a groan, he filled her. His hands held her bottom as he began a delicious rhythm. She wound her legs around his hips and closed her eyes, absorbing their oneness with every cell of her being.

All the sounds in the night blended, the wind outside the cabin, their breathing. The blankets were lost, tossed aside, and neither of them noticed; the cool air of the room was overpowered by the heat they generated.

Helplessly caught in the throes of passion, Tracy tossed her head, moaning. She was stunned by the degree of desire he drew from her again. Though it had been so easily sated moments ago, it was back, raging within her.

She gasped, clinging to him with almost savage tenacity, feeling the swirling, devouring delight again. She wanted to tell him not to hold back, but words were unnecessary and impossible. Together they reached the peak, climaxing in surging pleasure, each crying out, adding another facet of sound to the nightsong.

For long, peaceful moments they lay without moving. Then the coolness crept up on them, chilling their damp skin. Slade slipped from the bed, switched off the lamp and recovered the blankets, enclosing them both in a warm cocoon of entwined arms and soft flannel. His mouth was close to her ear. "You're the only woman I will ever want," he whispered huskily.

She was barely able to speak. "Even when I'm nine months pregnant and big as the horse barn," she teased, yawning.

"Even then." His hand went to her stomach and he caressed it gently. "It's a miracle, Tracy."

"I've always wanted children. Have you?" she asked drowsily.

In the dark, Slade frowned. That he hadn't dared hope for a woman like Tracy and children from her was much closer to the truth. He sighed, admitting the sad fact to himself. Then he pressed a kiss to Tracy's mouth. "Yes, I always wanted children. Go to sleep, sweetheart. You're exhausted."

"I guess I am. Good night, darling." Already she was half-asleep, and her voice was faint, husky.

The wind was getting stronger, blasting the cabin with mounting fury. Slade listened to it, remembering he hadn't banked the fire, and when Tracy was sleeping soundly he quietly got out of bed.

It took only a few minutes to tend the dying fire, and he returned to the bedroom and slid back beneath the blankets. Tenderly he curled around Tracy, burrowing his right arm under her pillow to get her as close to him as possible.

He vowed to never let her get very far away from him again. He fell asleep thinking of the long, wonderful years ahead of them.

Thirteen

Hours later, a strong wind still pelted the cabin's windows with bits of snow and ice, creating an almost pleasing cacophony. Slade had heard the sound hundreds of times in his life, and that wasn't what had brought him to sudden wakefulness. In fact, if he'd been the sort of person to feel fright at an abrupt middle-of-the-night alertness, he might have thought something unseen, or presently unheard, had drawn him from sleep. As it was, his heart was thudding unusually hard and his mouth felt dry. The only thing in his mind was Tracy—certainly no cause to awaken with a near-premonition of disaster.

She was deep under the blankets, curled into a ball of warm oblivion, and Slade could just make out the contrasting tones of her face and hair in the dark. To think she carried his child was a still-unbelievable treasure, and he softened as he watched her.

Maybe that was why he'd come so wide-awake. She hadn't agreed to marriage, had she?

Frowning, Slade went over the evening, first reliving the incredible satisfaction of their lovemaking, then working through her bombshell about the baby, lastly considering the story she'd related about his mother, Jason Moorland and Garve Hutchins, the man who was supposedly his real father.

Was it true? Tracy believed it to be. Obviously Rachel did, too, having provided Tracy with the information. And the journal was certainly clear on Jason Moorland's apparent—or imagined—sterility. The concept was pretty damned tough to accept, especially the part about Jemma relying on a lie her whole life to keep from telling her folks about Garve Hutchins.

Slade brought to mind the day he had asked Jemma point-blank for the story. Of course, he'd already heard a thousand times that his father was Jason Moorland. But for the first time he'd heard how the man had run out on a young, pregnant woman.

His eyes narrowed when he also recalled there had no longer been a reason to lie. Both of his grandparents had been dead for several years. He was sure Jemma Dawson hadn't been lying. Was Rachel's memory faulty? Or, dammit, was his?

Tracy was the one who needed to believe he wasn't her dead husband's son. Maybe nothing would ever convince him of that, even if his mother should somehow appear and renounce the tale he'd grown up with.

It was too ingrained, too much a part of what he was, for him to do a complete turnabout now.

Truthfully, he really didn't give a damn anymore. He wanted to start a new life, make his own happiness with Tracy and the baby.

If she allowed it.

Couldn't Tracy see what a good husband and father he intended to be? he wondered. He would love her and the child, take care of them, be there for them always. If only words came easier for him. If only he could find a way to make her know.

Sometime during the night, Tracy had moved from his arms. Now, her warmth radiated across a vacant span of several inches. Sighing, Slade closed the gap by curling around her again. Her skin was hot and satiny, and the contact brought an immediate renewal of desire. He slipped a hand between her arm and waist and slid it upward to her breasts, brushing his palm against the nipple.

He closed his eyes and let pure sensation fill his brain. Her complete femaleness was indisputable— and deeply arousing. Her curving feminine bottom in his lap brought him to immediate readiness, and he could no more prevent what he did next than stop himself from breathing. His hand glided down, down to the silky hair at the base of her abdomen.

He heard her sigh and come slowly awake as he explored, and the fact that she lay quietly and tempt-ingly relaxed her legs heightened the erotic moment. The blood pounded in his veins when he heard her breath quicken, and he raised his head to nip at an earlobe.

"Can you hear the storm?" he whispered. "We're having a real blizzard."

"Hmmm," was her deliciously husky reply.

"I love touching you. Do you mind being awakened like this?"

"Quite the opposite." She moved her hips sensuously.

Slade didn't know why he suddenly felt choked. "I'm going to love our baby, Tracy." He felt something intangible run through her body, a ripple, just the merest hint of a retreat. "Don't you believe me?" His hand moved to her waist.

Tracy turned onto her back. "I want to believe you. There's nothing I want more."

"But believing me doesn't come naturally, does it?"

"Slade, you show so little of yourself." She withdrew her hand from the blankets and touched his face. "I have such wonderful dreams," she said. "Dreams of you and me and the baby. But—"

"You're still afraid."

"Yes."

"If you don't marry me, what will you do? Will you let me see the baby?"

Her breath caught. "Of course you could see the baby. Slade, I'm not trying to hurt you in this. But a marriage without communication scares me to death."

Slade couldn't remember the last time he'd shed

tears. Even at his mother's death his grief had been private. Now humiliation racked him as he felt the searing heat of tears in his eyes. He cleared his throat and lay back with one arm crooked over his face, battling an urge he'd had very little experience with.

Sensing something amiss, Tracy pulled herself up on one elbow. "Slade? Are you all right?"

He felt his chest heave, and quickly, before she could see, he turned his back to her.

"Slade! What's wrong?" Concerned, Tracy leaned over him. Then she understood. He was weeping. Utterly amazed, she sat back. His shoulders were shaking, and for a moment she wasn't sure what to do.

But then, with tears in her own eyes, she wrapped her arms around him. "My poor darling," she whispered, realizing what was happening. The load had finally grown too cumbersome. Even a man as strong and independent as Slade had a breaking point, and he had reached his.

When he turned over suddenly and clutched her to him like a drowning man holding on to a life raft, her heart melted. He did need her. He was clinging to her as though his life depended on her. She had never heard a man cry so heartbreakingly before, and she wept along with him, stroking his back and trying to offer consolation, though her own tears made speaking clearly nearly impossible.

It only lasted a few minutes, but they were astonishingly meaningful minutes. When he finally quieted, she continued to hold him, to soothe him.

When he spoke, he sounded embarrassed. "I'm sorry. I don't know what came over me."

"Don't apologize," she said softly. "Not for being human, Slade."

"Men shouldn't cry."

"Oh? Do you think sensitivity should be reserved only for women? Slade, things just got to be too much for you. There's no shame in admitting that."

There was a box of tissues on the nightstand, and Slade sat up and grabbed a handful. He wiped his eyes and blew his nose, still so shaken emotionally that he wasn't sure he was through crying. Oddly, the first thing he said was, "I don't care anymore, Tracy. I don't care who my father is—or was. I'm through worrying about it."

"Is that why you wept?" She was lying back on her pillow, and her voice was quiet.

"I don't know. I don't know anything anymore."

"Have I confused you, Slade?" The bed rocked as he settled down again next to her.

"No! You're the only thing that makes any sense. I want you and our baby," he said hoarsely. "That's the one thing that's as clear as day."

"Then talk to me. Don't keep shutting me out."

"Talk about what? Those questions you raised earlier?"

"That would be a start. But those things only scratch the surface, Slade. You said you don't care anymore who your father is. Do you understand that it is important to me, and that it will be important to our child?"

"Yeah. I guess it would be, wouldn't it? I never thought of it that way. Dammit, Tracy, if she lied, why keep the lie going after my grandparents were gone?"

"Do you remember them?"

"Of course."

"Were they harsh people?"

"In a way, I suppose."

Tracy sighed. "Rachel said she felt your mother came to believe the lie. What do you think? Is that possible?"

"Hell, who knows? She talked all the time about how Jason Moorland was going to reappear one day. I know she believed that."

"Slade, do you believe the journal?"

"Moorland's sterility, you mean?"

"Yes."

"If it was true, why didn't he tell you?"

"You read what he wrote. He was afraid I wouldn't marry him."

"And you never suspected?"

"No. I think that's why I didn't worry about getting pregnant with you. I was all set to take some fertility tests before Jase died. I was positive there must be a physical reason why *I* didn't conceive."

"And good old Jason let you go right on thinking it, too, didn't he?"

"It was wrong, but yes, he did. I can't imagine what he would have done if I'd gone through the tests and proven I was fertile."

Slade gave a brief laugh. "Well, you're fertile, all

right. How many times did we make love before you conceived?''

''Three times—''

He turned toward her. ''I know how many times. That was a rhetorical question, sweetheart. Do you think I could forget one minute of our time together?'' He enclosed her in a warm embrace. ''You'll never find a man who loves you more,'' he whispered against her lips. ''Even if you don't know that I like country music and mystery novels.''

Tracy smiled. ''And your favorite color is blue.''

''On you.'' His mouth rested on hers for a moment, and when they separated again, his voice was serious. ''Tracy, I'll try so hard. I'll tell you everything. I'll talk so damn much you'll scream at me to shut up.''

''You? Now that would be the day,'' she said teasingly.

''Will you give me the chance to prove it? Don't judge me by my behavior last summer. Everything went haywire when I heard your name. One day, out of the blue—literally—appears the most gorgeous...'' He dropped a kiss on her mouth. ''...ravishing...'' he caught her lower lip between his and sucked gently. ''...sexy female I ever saw.''

She interjected, ''Only to be met by a glowering...'' in kind, she nipped at his lips ''—rude—'' her tongue flicked, tracing the curve of his bottom lip ''—sexy male.''

They laughed together. ''And then,'' Tracy continued, ''if that wasn't enough, that wild sexy man comes barreling through the bathroom door—''

"And stops dead in his tracks." Another kiss interrupted Slade's recitation, this one slightly longer in duration, a trifle more intense in feeling. "She was someone he'd only seen in his dreams," he finished softly. "Tracy, I nearly died when I saw you standing in that tub."

"Oh, sure, that's what you say now. You cad, you stared and stared."

Slade dug his hand beneath the blankets and lazily circled her breasts. "Want to know why?"

"Will you tell me?" Excitement was beginning to coil in her middle. This was different from anything they'd ever shared, playful but with sexual undertones. Her question was breathlessly stated.

"The minute I saw you I wanted to do this." Slade slid the blankets back and brought his mouth to a nipple. His lips encircled and his tongue swirled, enticing the sweet bud to an instant upright response.

Her eyes drifted shut, and her voice was husky. "Maybe I wanted you to do that, too," she whispered. "I hardly slept that night."

Slade grinned wickedly. "You wanted more than that, sweetheart. And if you'd been anyone other than Tracy Moorland you'd have gotten exactly what you wanted."

She laughed deep in her throat. "I wondered why you stopped. I couldn't figure it out. And I was so humiliated. I've never, ever behaved so wantonly."

The air changed when Slade took her lips in a long, heated kiss. He raised his head. "I came unglued when I touched you that night," he whispered.

"Why did you touch me? After our less-than-friendly beginning, it really surprised me."

Memory brought a dark shadow to Slade's mind. No, dammit, he wasn't going to hedge. Not ever again. Slade brought his head to the pillow. "I was being a total bastard," he confessed. "It started out as some kind of stupid revenge on Jason Moorland."

"Oh, Slade," she whispered. "I think I suspected something like that after I thought about it."

His hand caressed her hair. "But it didn't end that way. Actually, the laugh was on me. You might not have slept much before I got home, but I sure paid for it afterward. I had to get away from you. I couldn't count on being able to keep my hands to myself."

"And you came up here," she said.

"My hideaway." He chuckled softly. "Now it's *our* hideaway. At least for tonight," he added, suddenly very sober.

This was the kind of give-and-take she wanted between them—talk, laughter, honesty. This was all she asked. What had happened to alter things so drastically? Slade's emotional breakdown? Had a few minutes of tears breached his wall of privacy?

Tracy smiled with utter happiness. "I want to say something. Right this minute I feel very close to you. This is all I was trying to accomplish, Slade. You've been sharing yourself, and I haven't felt like an intruder. Can you tell the difference?"

"Sweetheart, I swear I'll never shut you out again. Do you believe me?"

"With all my heart," she whispered. "And I'll

never scream at you for talking too much. Not ever, ever, ever, " she added, a note of laughter in her voice.

"Are you saying what I think you're saying?" he asked cautiously.

Tracy moved up in the bed until she had one leg thrown across his lap and brought her lips to his.

A groan rose in Slade's throat, and his arms locked around her. Passion erupted, and speech was forgotten as the kiss deepened. With a sweet, sliding caress, Slade's hands moved to her hips, and he urged her on top of him, nestling her into the cradle of his thighs.

The storm raged beyond the cabin's foot-thick log walls, and within, Tracy heard the gusting with only partial awareness. She was encased within the warm flesh of hard, masculine arms and only a dim recognition of the elements outside the room developed in her mind. The seed of desire grew rapidly, radiating outward with liquid tentacles, creating a softness in her, a vulnerable openness. She wanted only to give to this man who could steal her strength and replace it with longing. His lips were a connection with life itself, and hers molded and shaped at his direction.

She felt a hand at the back of her head, entwined in her hair, and a tug upward. Her mouth left his. "You didn't tell me...did I interpret your message correctly?" he whispered hotly.

"You did," she replied breathlessly.

"You will marry me?"

A sudden coyness gripped her. "Ask me again."

"Again?" Slade reached for the lamp, stretching an arm upward, and the click of the switch bathed the bed in light. Tracy's hair was tumbled around her face, and there was a bit of surprise in her eyes, obviously over him wanting the light on. "I want to see you," he murmured. "No mistakes or misunderstandings this time, sweetheart."

She nodded, her heart thumping an accompaniment to the excitement she was feeling.

Slade took her face between his hands, planted a tender kiss on her lips and whispered, "I love you. Will you marry me?"

A smile was born. "Yes, I definitely will marry you."

"When?"

The smile broadened. "Sometime before May would be best, I think."

Slade attempted a serious expression. "How about tomorrow?"

Tracy laughed gleefully. "My, Montana males are impulsive."

"I've never been impulsive, and you know it!" Slade leaned over her. "Except right now I've got a mighty overpowering impulse." His expression showed his adoration. "I want to make love to you for hours," he whispered.

Her fingertips grazed his mouth. "Be my guest, darling," she teased, parting her lips for his kiss.

They stayed at the cabin for two wonderful days. Tracy glowed from making love, and also from the beautiful closeness developing between them. As Slade had declared, he was ready to talk, and he told her all about his childhood, his frustrations, his happy times, his sad times. He urged stories and confidences from her, too, once asking her if she could handle her business obligations from the ranch.

"I'm sure I can," she responded. "No doubt I'll have to go to San Francisco every so often, but you could go with me. That way we could combine business with pleasure."

"I'll go if you want."

"I want." She smiled.

They spoke of the Double J, and the plans Slade had been so reluctant to share before came spilling out, his dream of expanding the horse-breeding-and-training end of the business. Tracy became excited about it, immediately offering the money he needed, halting herself when she saw Slade become quiet.

Instantly she understood his reaction. She must watch herself, she realized. Slade was a very proud man, and her urging money on him every time he mentioned it wouldn't be wise. "Let me rephrase that," she said quietly. "I'd like to invest in your ideas. I think they're very sound, and I fell in love with the Thoroughbreds at first sight."

Slade relaxed. "I'm sorry. I got upset over nothing. I want you involved in the ranch. I want you involved in every part of my life."

That conversation ended in an incredible hour of lovemaking. But so did many others, and when they finally decided to leave the cabin, Tracy felt saturated with love.

On the way back to the ranch, however, Slade said the one thing that sealed her happiness.

The snow was deep, but they started out in bright sunshine, the sky so blue it was almost blinding. Bundled up again, Tracy rode Dolly with Slade watching the mare's every move. He was worried, Tracy knew, concerned that the horse might stumble or that she might somehow get jostled. Consequently they stopped often, with Slade checking the cinch, the saddle, every feature of the riding equipment, to make sure Tracy was safely mounted.

Their final stop before tackling the downward trail to the valley offered the most incredible view Tracy had ever seen. Awestruck by the immensity of the snowy scene below the hills, Tracy stared, wide-eyed. "Oh, Slade," she exclaimed. "You can see the entire ranch."

"And a few others, too," Slade laughed. "Not everything you see down there is part of the Double J."

"I suppose not, but, oh, my, it's lovely."

He helped her down, letting her slide easily through his arms, and Tracy moved a little closer to the edge of the bluff. "Don't go any farther," Slade cautioned immediately.

"I won't. Oh, this is so beautiful. Last summer I tried to picture the valley with snow."

Slade stepped up beside her and settled an arm around her shoulders. "Didn't you notice this view on the way up?"

Tracy smiled. "I had more on my mind than the scenic wonders of Montana," she admitted.

"I imagine you did." He squeezed her closer to himself. "I'm sure glad you're a tenacious little thing," he teased gently. "What if you had simply given up on me?"

"What if I hadn't decided to move and hadn't found those journals?" Tracy added with a shudder. "To think they'd been lying in that drawer all that time."

They stood in the wintry silence for a time, absorbing the vast scene before them. "Slade, you don't hold anything against Rachel, do you?" Tracy asked softly.

He drew a long breath. "I'm trying very hard not to."

"You know, she's the closest thing to a grandmother our baby will have."

"She'll be excited about it, I know," Slade replied.

"So will Dad. I'll call him when we get to the ranch."

"And invite him to the wedding?"

"Certainly. I think you'll like him, darling."

Slade grinned. "Will he like me?"

"I promise he will." She sighed from pure contentment. "What do you really want from the future?"

He never batted an eye. "You, the baby and the ranch," he answered at once.

Her heart leaped wildly. "In that order?"

"In exactly that order. If I had to make a choice

this minute, you or the Double J, I'd—'' a gleam entered his eyes ''—well, on second thought...''

"What?" Tracy heard the laughter in his voice and bent over to scoop up a handful of snow. Either he didn't believe she would really do it or he just wasn't quick enough—which Tracy doubted—because he gasped with surprise when she rubbed the snow in his face.

Then she ran—or tried to—giggling merrily. Her bulky clothing and the foot-deep snow made a hasty retreat impossible, and Slade easily caught her. "Wanna play, huh?" He threatened her with a gloveful of snow.

She was laughing, and then she wasn't. Slade had dropped the snow and was suddenly looking very romantic. His mouth drew near hers. "I'd rather play like this," he whispered, pressing his lips to hers in a heartwarming kiss. Then he groaned. "Too damned many clothes for fooling around, sweetheart." They brushed the snow from their clothing and laughed together. "Tonight I'll brave the balcony," he promised.

Before they remounted to continue the journey home, he held her. "I meant what I said, Tracy. There's no contest between you and anything else in the whole damn world, including the ranch."

Her eyes radiated emotion. "I love you, Slade Dawson."

He grinned. It was an endearing grin that lit his eyes. "And they lived happily ever after. You know, I think that line was invented for us, sweetheart."

"That it was, darling, that it was," she whispered, feeling the truth of it in her soul.

*   *   *   *   *

A LETTER FROM THE AUTHOR

Dear Reader,

What a thrill it is to have a book reissued, especially since *Big Sky Country* was my first published work.

As probably every author can attest, one question that keeps popping up is where do you get your ideas? Sometimes the question is accompanied by a sly glance at my husband, as though the adventure and romance in my stories just have to be Bill's doing. Well, some of it is. He's a great husband who's made me very happy for a good many years.

But even I don't know where some of my story lines come from. Sometimes it's a phrase that sticks in my mind, or a name, a picture, or a chat with my daughters. They have each helped me develop ideas—my mother, as well—and we've had a hilarious good time in the process.

Then there's my agent, Meg Ruley, who is always there to guide me over the rough spots. I will never forget the day she called me for the first time, soon after I had sent her some chapters of *Big Sky Country*. That was a once-in-a-lifetime experience.

And where would an author be without her editor? Lucia Macro was my first editor, and to say she was wonderful to a fledgling writer is a gross understatement. Thank you, Lucia.

I can only say that *Big Sky Country* came to life without any special reason, other than my wish to write a book set on a ranch in the West. After thirty books, it still remains one of my favorites. I hope you enjoy reading it as much as I enjoyed writing it.

Jackie Merritt

SILHOUETTE Romance™

Escape to a place where a kiss is still a kiss...
Feel the breathless connection...
Fall in love as though it were
the very first time...
Experience the power of love!

Come to where favorite authors——such as
Diana Palmer, Stella Bagwell,
Marie Ferrarella and many more——
deliver heart-warming romance and genuine
emotion, time after time after time....

Silhouette Romance——
stories straight from the heart!

Silhouette®
Where love comes alive™

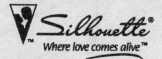

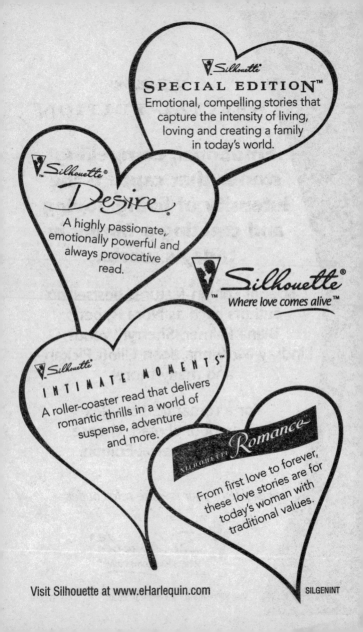